"You really ~~~~ ~~~~ ~~~~ing along?"

The disbelief in ~~~~ worse than a he~~~~ and he didn't have a thing against the boy, but in all honesty, he'd made the offer only to persuade Jazelle to go out with him. Well, that reason and the lost look in the boy's eyes. Connor had seen those same wary shadows whenever he'd looked at himself in the mirror and wondered why his own mother hadn't wanted him.

"I really don't mind," he told her.

She studied him for so long that he was finding it damned hard not to squirm.

Finally, she said, "Okay. We'll go."

He'd never imagined that three simple little words could make him so happy. "Great! I'll call you tomorrow and we'll figure out the time and place."

"Fine," she said. "Now, would you please let me get back to work?"

"Of course." Connor guided her over to the staircase, and as they descended the steps together, he wondered if he'd just won the lottery, or paddled his canoe straight into a stretch of white-water rapids.

* * *

MEN OF THE WEST:
Whether ranchers or lawmen, these heartbreakers
can ride, shoot—and drive a woman crazy!

Dear Reader,

When I first started writing about Three Rivers Ranch, a young woman in the background, quietly going about her job as housekeeper, caught my attention. Jazelle Hutton was the single mother to a very young son and completely devoted to him and the huge Hollister family. She was always working tirelessly for others, rather than herself, and I began to wonder about her life. How had she come to be on the huge ranch in the first place? And why didn't she have someone special in her life? Before long, I realized that Jazelle deserved her own story, but the Hollister siblings kept pushing her out of the way.

Thankfully, Jazelle's turn finally arrived, and it's been a real joy revealing her hopes and sorrows, and her dreams for herself and her little son, Raine. Although, I have to admit, I never imagined for one minute that she'd take a second look at Deputy Sheriff Connor Murphy. True, he'd been a lifelong friend of Joseph Hollister, but he was a known womanizer and as far away from a family man as Earth to Mars. Falling for him could only mean heartache. Or would it?

I hope you'll enjoy reading how these two wounded hearts come together and Raine gets the daddy he's always wanted.

God bless the trails you ride,

Stella Bagwell

Her Man Behind the Badge

STELLA BAGWELL

HARLEQUIN
SPECIAL
EDITION

HARLEQUIN®
SPECIAL EDITION™

Recycling programs
for this product may
not exist in your area.

ISBN-13: 978-1-335-89473-1

Her Man Behind the Badge

Copyright © 2020 by Stella Bagwell

This edition published by arrangement with Harlequin Books S.A.

For questions and comments about the quality of this book,
please contact us at CustomerService@Harlequin.com.

Harlequin Enterprises ULC
22 Adelaide St. West, 40th Floor
Toronto, Ontario M5H 4E3, Canada
www.Harlequin.com

Printed in U.S.A.

After writing more than one hundred books for Harlequin, **Stella Bagwell** still finds it exciting to create new stories and bring her characters to life. She loves all things Western and has been married to her own real cowboy for forty-four years. Living on the south Texas coast, she also enjoys being outdoors and helping her husband care for the horses, cats and dog that call their small ranch home. The couple has one son, who teaches high school mathematics and is also an athletic director. Stella loves hearing from readers. They can contact her at stellabagwell@gmail.com.

Books by Stella Bagwell

Harlequin Special Edition

Men of the West

The Arizona Lawman
Her Man on Three Rivers Ranch
A Ranger for Christmas
His Texas Runaway
Home to Blue Stallion Ranch
The Rancher's Best Gift

The Fortunes of Texas: Rambling Rose

Fortune's Texas Surprise

The Fortunes of Texas: The Lost Fortunes

Guarding His Fortune

Montana Mavericks: The Lonelyhearts Ranch

The Little Maverick Matchmaker

Visit the Author Profile page
at Harlequin.com for more titles.

To all those brave lawmen who dedicated their lives to bringing law and order to the untamed West.

Chapter One

Connor Murphy fastened the seat belt across his broad chest and darted a glance at the dark landscape whizzing by the passenger window of the truck.

"In case you've forgotten, Joe, the sheriff's office is in the opposite direction. And there's no sense in you getting the idea that we're a two-man posse tonight," he added with weary sarcasm. "The thieves who burgled the Wallace house are probably over in California by now."

"Wrong. We'll find the rats right around Wickenburg. And soon," Joseph Hollister replied. "Right now I want to make another stop. Jazelle, the woman who works as the housekeeper for my family on Three Rivers Ranch, lives right over this next rise.

I want to make sure her place wasn't hit by the same thieves."

Connor groaned. "Damn, Joe, don't you think she would've already called the sheriff's office and reported it? We're not riding horses down the main street in Tombstone and you're not Wyatt Earp." He jabbed a finger in the direction of the radio built into the dash of the truck. "These days we have instant communication and transportation."

"So we do," Joseph said, unaffected by Connor's grumbling. "But Jazelle often has to work late at Three Rivers. She might not even be home yet. At least we can look around and make sure the doors and windows are all intact."

The two men had already pulled a sixteen-hour shift and Connor was dog tired. He wanted to go home, drink a beer and fall into bed. But he wasn't going to argue with Joe. The man wasn't just his work partner, he'd been a close friend since childhood and Connor had learned long ago that it was next to impossible to win an argument with the man.

Scowling, Connor asked, "Doesn't this woman have a husband to see after things?"

"No. And she's always too busy taking care of everyone at Three Rivers to have time to do much at her own place."

Connor sighed. "Okay. But let's make this safety check snappy. I'm about to fall flat on my face."

"Right." Joseph glanced at him and chuckled. "What you need, Connor, is two kids and a wife to go home to. They'd make you forget all about being tired."

He cocked an eyebrow at Joseph then snorted. "Sure, Joe. If I thought I had to go home to a nagging wife and a pair of screaming kids, you'd have to send the law out looking for me."

Joseph grinned. "Tessa doesn't nag. And my kids don't scream—well, only when they're mad about something."

Connor didn't bother to reply. He couldn't dispute a man who was deeply in love with his wife and doted on the son and daughter she'd given him. And that was well and good, Connor thought. He was glad for his friend. But that kind of life wasn't for him. No way in hell.

Joseph flipped on the turn signal and steered the truck to a stop behind a ten-year-old Ford truck with faded red paint. "Looks like Jazelle is home. If we're lucky, she might have noticed something as she drove by the Wallace place."

On a small planked porch flanked by two gnarled juniper trees, Joseph knocked on the door of the little stucco house. Connor stood to one side and peered around the dark yard.

"The woman needs a yard light," Connor observed. "You couldn't see a prowler around here if he walked two feet in front of you."

Joseph frowned. "Yeah. I'll talk to Mom. She'll send a couple of the ranch hands out to put one up for her."

Since the Hollisters owned and operated Three Rivers Ranch—one of the biggest cattle and horse ranches in the entire state of Arizona—they didn't lack for money. Erecting a yard light would be penny ante stuff for them.

With no sound coming from inside the house, Joseph knocked again.

"I don't think she's going to come to the door, Joe. It's after ten. She's probably already gone to bed."

Connor had barely gotten the words out of his mouth when a light suddenly flooded the porch, followed by the rattle of the latch. As the wooden door finally creaked open, Connor peered around Joseph's right shoulder to see a very young woman with long blond hair standing on the threshold.

She stared at the two men in stunned fascination. "Joe! What are you doing here? Is something wrong at the ranch?" she asked anxiously.

Joseph quickly held up a hand to allay her fears. "Don't worry, Jazelle. Everything at the ranch is fine. Actually, we're here to check on you."

"Me? I don't understand." She pushed the door wide and gestured for the two deputies to enter. "Please, come in."

Connor followed Joseph inside, stepping to one side and waiting as the woman shut the door then came around to stand in front of them.

Clearly confused by their visit, her gaze vacillated between Connor and Joseph. "Okay, now tell me why I needed to be checked on. Did someone report me driving erratically in town or something?"

It was a good thing Joseph chose to do the explaining because, for once in his life, Connor wasn't sure he could form a cohesive sentence if his life depended on it. This woman was too young and pretty and downright sexy to be the Hollisters' housekeeper!

"Nothing like that. And don't be alarmed," Joseph told her, "but your neighbor's house was broken into tonight. You didn't notice anything amiss at their place on your way home, did you?"

Shocked, she said, "Oh, no! Were the Wallaces home when it happened? Was anyone hurt?"

Joseph said, "They were gone at the time of the break-in. Some valuables were taken."

Connor barely heard the conversation between Joseph and the blonde. He was too busy staring and too stunned to hear much of anything being said. Like an idiot, he'd been expecting a stereotypical middle-aged woman with a thick waist, tightly permed hair and crepe-soled shoes. Instead, this woman could hardly be past twenty-five. Her blond hair was sleek and smooth, and hung far below her shoulder blades. Bare toes, sporting bright pink nail polish, peeped out from beneath the frayed hems of her faded blue jeans.

"That's awful!" she exclaimed. Then, with a rueful shake of her head, added, "Sorry, Joe, but I didn't drive by the Wallaces' tonight. I had to pick up a few things in town, so I drove home from the opposite direction."

"I see. Well, I thought I'd ask just in case."

The woman named Jazelle looked straight at him and Connor felt a surge of energy suddenly sweep away his fatigue.

Stepping forward, he said, "Since Joe hasn't seen fit to introduce us, I'm his partner, Connor Murphy."

She offered her hand to him and Connor was quick to wrap his around her soft, slender fingers.

"Nice to meet you, Mr. Murphy. I'm Jazelle Hutton."

There wasn't a speck of makeup on her face and yet it was full of rich color, he noted. Her eyes were a warm brown that made him think of caramel and coffee all mixed together. Slanted cheekbones held a hint of pink, while her plush lips looked as though she'd been eating raspberries.

"Make it Connor," he said, thinking there was nothing shy about this woman. Not with the way she was making direct eye contact with him.

"All right, Connor. And I'm Jazelle to everyone."

Totally bemused, he continued to stare at her lovely face. She stared back just long enough for him to draw a deep breath before she cleared her throat and eased her hand from his.

From the corner of his eye, Connor could see Joseph casting him a droll look. But it would hardly be the first time his partner had shot him a hands-off warning.

Joseph turned his keen gaze away from Connor to survey the small living room with its wooden floor, braided rugs and beige walls adorned with framed photos and paintings. "Since you arrived home, have you discovered anything missing?" he asked.

"No," Jazelle told him. "But I've not been here long enough to really notice."

"What about open windows or doors?" Connor asked, cringing at the thought of thieves breaking in on this vulnerable beauty. Would she know how to protect herself?

"None of that. I entered the house through the back door and it was still locked," she said and then glanced questioningly at Joseph. "Are you thinking these creeps might come back to this area?"

Since Jazelle Hutton lived on a lonely country road a few miles east of town, Connor figured her house and the Wallace place would always be targets. But he didn't want to voice his opinion and scare the lady.

"Hard to say, Jazelle," Joseph replied. "Just be sure to keep everything locked up. I really think you ought to get a dog. One that would bark if anyone drove up."

"Oh, Joe, I'm not here long enough to warrant having a dog," she said. "It wouldn't be fair to the poor animal staying here by itself all the time. No. I'll just keep a can of Mace by the bed."

Connor was about to suggest a weapon stronger than Mace when the sound of pattering footsteps had him glancing toward an open doorway on the far side of the room.

A towheaded boy, somewhere near five or six years of age, and dressed in striped pajamas, stumbled sleepily into the room.

"Raine! What are you doing out of bed?" Jazelle asked as the boy sidled up to her leg.

Using both fists to rub his eyes, he mumbled, "I heard you talking, Mommy."

Joseph said, "Sorry, Jazelle. We didn't mean to wake your son."

Mommy. Your son. This boy was hers! Connor didn't want to believe it was true. Especially since he had a steadfast policy never to be interested in a woman with a child. Keeping things simple and uncomplicated with the women he dated was difficult enough without bringing a child into the equation. No thanks. Blond beauty or not, as far as he was concerned, Jazelle had just slipped off his romance radar.

The boy must have recognized Joseph's voice because he suddenly dropped his fists and looked at the two deputies.

"Uncle Joe!" he cried and raced toward Joseph.

Connor watched his partner squat and gather the boy in a tight hug. "How's my boy?"

The child leaned back and patted Joseph's cheek. "I'm good. Why are you here? It's dark outside," he asked, "and you have your badge on."

Smiling, Joseph reached up and pushed a thick

hank of blond hair off Raine's forehead. "Well, my partner and I just happened to be driving by and we thought we'd stop and say hello to your mommy."

Connor glanced over at Jazelle and saw a look of relief pass over her face. Obviously she hadn't wanted her son frightened by the thought of bad men coming into the house. He could tell just by the gentle way she looked at her son, that she was one of those mothers who'd fight like a wildcat to protect her child. Too bad his mother hadn't held those same protective instincts, Connor thought ruefully. Hell, it was too bad he'd never had a mother period.

"Oh." Raine glanced suspiciously at Connor and asked, "What's your name?"

Moving a step closer, he gave the boy a friendly smile. "My name is Connor. What's yours?"

"Raine. And I'm this many." Easing away from Joseph's hug, he turned to Connor and held up five fingers. "I went to kindergarten all day long, too. But it's summer now, so I don't have to go to school."

"Wow! All day. You're going to be a smart boy with all that learning."

"I'm already smart. That's what Mommy tells me."

Joseph laughed while Jazelle let out a good-natured groan.

"Then you're going to be even smarter," Connor told the child, glancing over to see his mother's face had turned a dull pink.

"Come here, Raine," she said. "We need to let

Joe and Connor be on their way. They have more deputy work to do. And it's time for you to get back into bed."

The boy trotted to his mother's side and Connor followed Joseph to the door.

"See you two later," Joseph said.

Connor glanced over his shoulder at the woman and the boy. "And be sure to lock up behind us," he told her then winked at Raine. "'Bye, Raine."

"'Bye," the boy said shyly.

Jazelle smiled at Connor and, in spite of his watch reading a quarter to eleven, he could've sworn the sun had just come out.

"I'll do it right now," she said.

As they stepped off the porch, Connor could hear her bolt the door behind them. He was relieved that she was taking precautions to keep herself and her son safe. But he was hardly relieved at the strange feelings that had been flashing through him ever since he'd laid eyes on Jazelle Hutton.

From time to time, he'd heard Joseph speak of their housekeeper, but he'd never met her personally. In fact, Connor hadn't been out to Three Rivers in a long while. Not since he and Joseph began putting in long work hours.

"That was certainly a surprise," Connor said as the two men climbed back into the truck. "Why didn't you tell me about Jazelle Hutton before now?"

Frowning, Joseph started the engine and put the gearshift into Reverse. "What do you mean 'tell you about her'? You've heard me talk about our house-keeper. Well, she's not my housekeeper any more since Tessa and I live on the Bar X," he corrected himself, "but she's a part of the family on Three Rivers."

Connor wiped a hand over his face as fatigue began to flood back into every muscle in his body. "That's not what I mean. Why didn't you tell me she was young and beautiful?"

There was a long pause and then Joseph shook his head. "You have plenty of women in Yavapai County without Jazelle."

Frowning, Connor glanced at him. "We're the same age, Joe. So why do you always have to treat me like you're the big brother?"

He shrugged. "Just bossy, I guess. Anyway, Jazelle's been with the family for seven years or so now. She's like a sister to me. I guess the times you've visited the ranch she wasn't around. Otherwise, you would've probably seen her."

The moment Connor had seen her standing in the doorway, questions had started swimming around in his head. Why was a lovely woman like her single? Where was the father of her child?

"Seven years…" Connor repeated thoughtfully. "She must have been mighty young when she started working for your family."

"Eighteen. Just out of high school."

So that made her twenty-five now, Connor thought. Eight years younger than him. He'd never let age stand in the way of a beautiful woman before. Still, he couldn't forget about the boy. His policy of not dating a single mother was a good one. It kept him out of messy entanglements and made it easy when the time came to say goodbye.

"What about Raine's dad? Is he around?"

"No. And good riddance, I'd say. Chandler met him once, but I never did. He was a day hand on the Johnson Ranch. I'm not sure what happened between him and Jazelle, or why it didn't work out. All I know is that the guy was out of her life long before Raine was born. That was about a year after she'd come to work on Three Rivers."

Connor was suddenly thinking of the heartache and hardship Jazelle must have endured because of the shiftless cowboy. And then there was little Raine with his round, freckled face and big blue eyes. He'd never know his biological father. Connor was surprised at how much that fact bothered him. Unfortunately, there were plenty of kids around without a father or a mother. In his line of work, he saw many of them.

"Uh, does Jazelle have a special guy in her life now?"

A scowl wrinkled Joseph's forehead. "I don't think so. I've heard Mom remark that Jazelle is carrying around too many scars to ever want another man in her life. Sometime back, my sister Vivian tried to set her up with a park ranger she works with, but Jazelle flatly refused to meet him."

Sounded like Jazelle wasn't interested in dating or in finding a father for Raine. Well, he could hardly blame her. She'd been burned in the worst kind of way. Yet he couldn't help thinking that she was too young and lovely to go through life alone. And that little boy could sure use the comforting hand of a father.

"She's not your type."

The last of Joseph's words tugged Connor out of his rambling thoughts and he frowned at his buddy. "Who's not my type?"

"Damn. You are tired. Who do you think? We were talking about Jazelle."

Trying not to bristle, Connor replied, "I never said she was my type. Why would you even bother saying such a thing? You know I don't go out with women who have children."

"Jazelle only has one child."

"One is all it takes for me to push on the brakes." Connor leaned his head against the headrest and closed his burning eyes. "But he's a cute little guy."

"You don't even have enough patience to get along with your cat much less a child."

Connor didn't bother opening his eyes. "That damned tom doesn't want to get along with anyone or anything," he muttered. "He only stops by once in a while to beg for a meal. And don't be worrying about my lack of patience. I don't want to be a father now. Or ever."

"Okay. Got it. As far as you're concerned, Jazelle

is off limits," Joseph muttered. "For her sake, I hope you remember that."

Connor scowled. "You know just the right button to push to make me feel about two inches tall. Well, go ahead. Remind me that I'm a sorry son of a gun. At least I recognize my limitations."

"Is that what you call them?"

Ignoring the sarcasm in Joseph's voice, Connor let out a tired grunt. "Look, partner, I've already forgotten Jazelle and her son. I have a date tomorrow night with a luscious little redhead. That's what I have to look forward to."

Joseph sighed. "One of these days, Connor, you're going to end up crying in your beer."

No, he thought, his partner was wrong. Connor would never shed a single tear over a woman, or child, or anything else. The last time he'd cried, he'd been fifteen years old and he'd watched his father's lifeless body being carried away in the back of a hearse. Since then, his eyes had dried and his heart had hardened. He no longer knew how to cry.

Chapter Two

"Mommy, why was Uncle Joe here at our house? Is he chasing bad people?" Raine asked, tugging on the leg of his mother's jeans.

Jazelle took her son by the shoulders and turned him in the direction of the bedroom. She regretted that he'd awoken to find the two deputies in the living room. But thankfully both men had been thoughtful enough to keep the real reason for their visit from her son.

"Where did you hear that Joe chases bad people?" she asked.

"Grandma Reeva says so."

Reeva was the longtime family cook at Three Rivers Ranch. For the past seven years, Jazelle had worked closely with the older woman and, over time, she'd become like a second mother to her and more of a grandmother to Raine than his actual grandmother, Della Hutton.

"Well, sometimes it's Joe's job to chase bad men," Jazelle told him. "But not tonight. Joe and his partner just happened to drive by our house, so they stopped to say hello. That's all."

She disliked bending the truth, but at Raine's age, he didn't need to know that thieves had been prowling the home of their nearest neighbors. It would only frighten him.

The boy's small bedroom was modestly furnished with a twin-size bed, a chest of drawers and a nightstand with a lamp. The walls were covered with colorful posters of horses and dinosaurs. In one corner, a wooden box was filled with an assortment of toys ranging from dump trucks and race cars to baseballs and stuffed animals.

Raine headed straight to the rumpled bed. Halfway there, he paused to look back at his mother. "I wish Little Joe had been with Uncle Joe. Can we go see Little Joe tomorrow, Mommy? And baby Spring?"

Jazelle pulled back the rumpled covers on the bed. Raine leaped onto the mattress and snuggled his head on the pillow. As she smoothed the sheet and a light blanket over him, she said, "Not tomorrow. But we'll stop by the Bar X and see them soon. You like to play with Little Joe and Spring, don't you?"

"Yeah! We have fun!" he exclaimed with a toothy grin. Then, just as quickly, his little face took on a thoughtful expression. "Little Joe is Spring's brother. And she's his sister. Did you know that, Mommy?"

"Yes, I did." But she had no idea that Raine thought of the two children in the terms of being relatives.

Wondering if she should say more on the subject, Raine spoke again. "Uncle Joe is their daddy, too. And Little Joe says it's fun to have a daddy. 'Cause I asked him. Is it, Mommy?"

Her throat suddenly tight with emotions, Jazelle tucked the sheet beneath his armpits. "Is it what?"

"Fun to have a daddy?"

How could she answer her son's question? The man who'd fathered Raine had never been in his life. Nor would he ever be. In fact, other than one grainy photo, Raine had never seen the man. Her son didn't know what having a father in the house meant or the difference it might make to him.

As for Jazelle, she'd been in junior high school when a divorce had split her parents. Afterward, her father had moved two hundred miles away and she'd rarely had the opportunity to spend time with him since.

Taking a seat on the edge of the mattress, Jazelle gently smoothed a hand through Raine's tawny blond hair. "Well, it was fun when I was a little girl and Dad—your grandpa Sherman— was home. He liked to laugh and sing a lot."

"I heard him laugh and sing one time," Raine said. "But we don't see him very much."

"No. Your grandpa is very busy working in the mine." And taking care of the wife and two children he'd acquired after leaving Jazelle and her mother behind.

She could honestly say she didn't blame or resent her father for making a new life for himself. While her parents had been married, he'd tried hard to make Jazelle's mother happy. But Della was the sort of woman who'd never allow herself to be cheery or positive about anything. It would've been a major mistake for Sherman to remain in such an intolerable marriage.

"If I ever have a daddy, I want him to be nice like Uncle Joe. I don't want a mean one."

Jazelle blinked at the moisture stinging the backs of her eyes. "Raine, I promise that I will never let anyone be mean to you. Not ever. Okay?"

Grinning, he raised up and wrapped his arms around Jazelle's neck. "I love you, Mommy. Lots and lots."

"I love you, too, honey." She swallowed hard as she eased his head back against the pillow and pressed a kiss on his forehead. "Go to sleep now. And in the morning, you can go to the ranch with me."

His grin was wide. "I don't have to go to Kiddy Korner tomorrow?"

Smiling, Jazelle touched her forefinger to the tip of his nose. "No. You don't have to go to Kiddy Korner. Reeva and I are going to be doing some extra baking and tomorrow is Kat's workday, so you can help me watch the twins. How's that?"

"Good!" he said then giggled. "Abby and Andy are funny 'cause they do naughty things."

Blake Hollister, the eldest of the Hollister siblings, and his wife, Katherine, had three-year-old twins and a thirteen-year-old son, Nick. Chandler, the second eldest brother of the bunch, along with his wife, Roslyn, and their two babies, Evelyn, who was going on three and one year old, Billy, also lived in the big ranch house.

When Jazelle had first started her job at Three Rivers Ranch, none of the Hollister siblings had been married. Now the four brothers and two sisters all had wives and husbands and young children to round out their families. Along the way, "part-time nanny" had been added to Jazelle's duties of housekeeper and kitchen help. But she didn't mind the extra work. She loved children and the Hollisters were more like her family to her than her actual relatives were.

Tickling Raine beneath his chin, she said, "Well, you just make sure you don't do any naughty things, young man."

He giggled again as Jazelle turned off the bedside lamp and switched on a tiny night-light.

"Good night, funny bones."

"'Night, Mommy."

Jazelle left the bedroom door partially open and walked out to the kitchen to make sure the back door was securely locked. She'd lived alone in this same little house since she was eighteen years old and she'd never felt uneasy. The rural area outside of Wickenburg had always been quiet and safe. Still, she couldn't deny that the break-in at the Wallace house left her a little shaken.

Feeling more restless than she cared to admit, she walked out to the living room and rechecked the lock on the front door. Satisfied it was bolted, she plopped into a wooden rocker and switched on the television just to have a bit of noise in the house. After a moment, the screen flickered to the Phoenix evening news, where a weatherman was pointing to a blazing sun icon plastered over several counties. Like three-digit temperatures were anything new for August in Arizona.

Closing her eyes, she put the rocker into a gentle motion and tried to relax. But her plan was instantly waylaid as the image of Connor Murphy suddenly paraded through her thoughts.

Before tonight, she'd heard his name mentioned in connection with Joseph's work, but she'd never met the man. Tall, and nothing but lean muscle, the deputy had looked every inch the rough, tough lawman. Beneath his gray Stetson, his thick blond hair curled slightly around his ears and against the back of his neck. His face, burned brown by the sun, had a squared jaw, hard-chiseled lips and eyes bluer than the azure sky.

When he'd introduced himself, those eyes had

looked at her with a soft sort of gleam. And if that hadn't been enough to scatter her senses, he'd held on to her hand for what had seemed like ages. During that span of actual seconds, however, all she'd been able to think about was how warm and callused his palm felt against hers, and how those masculine lips curved into the most beguiling smile she'd ever seen on any man.

At some point during the visit, Jazelle had suffered a brain lapse and it wasn't until the two men had left and Raine had tugged on the leg of her jeans that she'd finally managed to pull herself together.

Now that she was thinking rationally again, common sense told her that a long line of women probably always trailed after him. And from the empty ring finger on his left hand, none had so far managed to catch him. That was hardly a surprise.

Guys like Connor Murphy were the fun-loving sort. Not the kind who wanted a wife and children to go home to. He was also the type of man that Jazelle would walk a mile to avoid, so she didn't need to give him one more minute of thought. As far as that went, she didn't need to waste her time thinking about any man. She was just fine without one.

Little Joe says it's fun to have a daddy. Is it, Mommy?

Raine's question shot a pang of regret through Jazelle and, with a weary sigh, she switched off the TV and rose from the rocker. Maybe she was just fine without a man in her life, but her son wasn't. He was missing so, so much because she'd not been woman enough to hold on to his father. Because, even now, after all these years, she was still too cowardly to consider giving Raine a stepfather and siblings.

Damn it, what in heck was wrong with her? Just because a good-looking deputy had shaken her hand and smiled at her, she'd suddenly gone all emotional. She didn't have time for such nonsense. Tomorrow was going to be a heavy workday at the ranch. She needed to be in bed, getting as much rest as she could, not thinking about a blond-haired deputy who had "playboy" written all over him.

With that mindset, she turned off the lights and headed straight to the bathroom for a quick shower.

She'd just pulled on a pair of light cotton pajamas and was combing out her damp hair when her cell phone rang. Puzzled that someone would be calling at such a late hour, she snatched up the phone from the nightstand and glanced at the ID illuminated on the screen. Seeing it was Joseph's wife, she immediately swiped to answer.

"Jazelle! For a minute, I thought you weren't going to answer," Tessa said with a rush of relief. "Have you already gone to bed?"

"No. Just getting ready. Is anything wrong?" Jazelle asked. They had been friends ever since the young woman had moved from Nevada to her late father's ranch, the Bar X, which was located only a few miles from Three Rivers Ranch.

"I'm calling just to make sure everything is okay

there. Joe just came in a few minutes ago and told me about the break-in at your neighbor's house."

Jazelle sat on the edge of the bed. "All is quiet here. The doors and windows are locked, and I'll keep an ear out."

"Keep your phone right beside you, Jazelle," Tessa ordered. "If you hear anything, punch Joe's number. We're closer to you than the nearest deputy station. He can be there in a matter of minutes. Promise you will."

She tried to laugh, but the sound was a bit shaky even to her own ears. "Tessa, you're being paranoid. The thieves would have to be downright stupid to hit this area twice in a matter of hours."

"Criminals are stupid, Jazelle. That's why they're criminals."

Jazelle could hardly argue the point. "Okay. I promise. But don't worry about me and Raine. We'll be fine."

Tessa wasn't the least bit reassured. "What I really wish is that you and Raine would go stay at Three Rivers tonight. Or better yet, just stop here at the Bar X and stay with us. We have plenty of room for you two."

"Thanks, dear friend, for your concern, but we're staying right here at home."

Tessa sighed. "Okay—I give up. You're staying home. I can't say that I blame you. But I will worry. Call me early in the morning—as soon as you get up."

"Tessa, that's at four thirty." And even at that early

hour, she barely had time to throw on her clothes and make the drive to Three Rivers by five.

"I know. That's just about the time Spring wants her diaper changed. I'll be awake."

Jazelle chuckled. "I promise I'll call. Now get off the phone and visit with your husband while you have the chance."

"I'm heating his supper as we speak," she said. "So—oh, before I hang up, what did you think about Connor?"

Jazelle lifted the phone away and stared comically at the screen before she finally returned it to her ear. "What did I think? Is this some kind of trick question?"

Tessa laughed. "Not hardly. Joe said that Connor introduced himself to you, so I wondered what kind of impression you had of him. Remember, I've told you he's single."

For some idiotic reason, Jazelle felt her heart thump just a tad faster. "I remember. You also told me he eats women for breakfast then spits them out before his midmorning snack."

Another burst of laughter came over the phone. "I said no such thing! I said he likes women. In the plural sense."

"Well, that's his own business and none of mine."

"You thought he was good-looking, huh?"

No, he was more than good-looking. He was a hot, hot hunk of man. That's what Jazelle actually thought, but Tessa would be the last person she'd utter those words to. Sooner or later, her friend would tell Joseph and then the paraphrase would eventually be relayed to Connor. And that would be worse than embarrassing.

"I'm sure most women would think so. I don't have time for such…things."

Tessa groaned. "More like you don't have the 'want to.' Well, in Connor's case, it's probably a good thing that you're gun-shy. I seriously doubt you could tame the man."

That stung. And Jazelle figured her friend had meant it to. "Why would I want to?"

"Oh, I don't know. Could be you're getting tired of a cold, empty bed. That you're tired of Raine not having a father to love and guide him. That you'd like to have a man standing next to you."

Jazelle frowned. "Tessa, are you pregnant again?"

Tessa's chuckle was a bit cunning. "Why are you asking me that question? Am I looking pudgy?"

"I haven't seen you in a couple of weeks and you looked like your beautiful svelte self then. No, I'm asking because you're talking crazy—like you're on hormone overload."

Her chuckle turned into a dreamy sigh. "That's what living with Joe does to me. I can't wait to have another baby."

"And Joe?"

"He can't wait to give me one."

The tender yearning she heard in Tessa's voice reminded Jazelle of the feelings she sometimes experienced in the deepest, loneliest part of the night. A longing to be connected to a man she loved. To conceive his baby and see the child gently cradled in his arms.

Clearing the tightness from her throat, she said, "Then I'll keep my fingers crossed that you both get your wish."

"Thank you, dear friend. And promise me you'll stay on alert."

"I promise. See you soon."

Jazelle ended the call and, after placing the phone on the nightstand, went back to removing the damp tangles from her hair.

Once her hair was hanging smooth against her back, she climbed into bed and turned off the light. But switching off her churning thoughts wasn't quite so easy.

You thought he was good-looking, huh?

The question had caught her completely off guard. It wasn't like Tessa to mention a man from a romantic viewpoint. Her friend understood just how scarred Jazelle had been when Spence had ended their relationship and gone back to his former fiancée. Jazelle had been brokenhearted, pregnant, and more alone than she'd ever been in her life.

Living in a small town, she'd felt as though everyone had been pointing fingers and laughing at how stupid and gullible she'd been to trust a drifting cowboy. Even her own mother had turned her back on her. In fact, Della continued to remind Jazelle of all the foolish mistakes she'd made by jumping into bed with a worthless man. And her daughter would carry those mistakes the rest of her life.

Maybe that was true, Jazelle thought sadly. The stigma of being a jilted woman and a single mother might always follow her. But at least Raine would grow up knowing that his mother loved him more than anything. At least Jazelle could hold her head up and truthfully say that all the choices she'd made since her son had been born had been made for her child's sake and never her own.

Looking into Connor Murphy's eyes and feeling the slightest twinge of attraction was not among the rules Jazelle had set for herself. And she wasn't about to start breaking those rules now. Even for a sexy deputy with a smile that outshone the sun.

Five days later, Connor and Joseph were sitting at their desks in the small workspace they shared at the sheriff's office, typing up the last of an arrest report. Earlier that morning, the two men had collared the pair of thieves who'd broken into the Wallace home and had even managed to recover part of the stolen items.

"I feel damned good about putting those two losers behind bars," Connor said. "I just wish we'd found Mrs. Wallace's jewelry among the things we recovered from that toolshed. But I figure the rings and necklaces were the first things to go to a pawn shop."

"Probably headed to Maricopa County with it. We'll check the pawn shops, but you and I both know it would be a long shot to find the jewelry now."

"Yeah. About a thousand to one." Connor punched the save button on his computer then left his desk to pour himself a cup of coffee from the machine stashed in one corner of the room.

While he stirred in a hefty amount of powdered creamer, Joseph picked up the desk phone and rapidly punched in a number.

"Are you calling Dan's?" Connor asked, referring to one of the pawnshops they usually first questioned when jewelry was involved in a robbery.

"No. I'm calling the ranch," Joseph answered before directing his attention back to the phone. "Reeva, Joe here. Is Jazelle around?" He paused to listen then said, "Oh, the babies. Yeah, I can imagine. Billy screams like a banshee. Well, can you ring that upstairs phone? I'd like to speak with her directly. No. Nothing is wrong. Everything is good. Okay. Thanks, Reeva."

The mention of Jazelle's name caused Connor to pause in his tracks. For the past five days, he'd been pestered by the image of the housekeeper and her little boy. Against his better judgment, he wanted to see her again. In fact, he'd considered stopping by her place in the guise of a safety check, but had decided that would look far too obvious.

And, anyway, he needed to steer clear of the

woman, Connor thought as he sat in the rolling desk chair and propped his feet out in front of him.

"That's right," Joseph was saying into the phone. "Connor and I wanted you to know—so you can rest easy. Sure. I will. 'Bye."

He hung up and glanced over at Connor. "Jazelle sounded relieved that we got the creeps. Frankly, I am, too. Most likely they wouldn't have targeted her house, but you never know."

Connor said, "I noticed there was a hill that hid her house from the road. Makes her place a little isolated. She lives too far from Wickenburg to be protected by the city police. And not close enough to any of the sheriff department's four command stations to get quick help."

"She's in a vulnerable spot," Joseph agreed. "Tessa worries about her and Raine. Which is kinda funny... Before we were married, Tessa lived on the Bar X alone and she thought I was being ridiculous for worrying about her safety."

"Well, you did suggest that Jazelle get a dog, and she shot down that idea," Connor replied.

Joseph shrugged. "Jazelle was right. She stays out at the ranch so much that the dog would practically be living alone. And dogs are like humans. They're not meant to be alone."

"Who says? I've lived alone for years."

Joseph grimaced. "Yeah, but who says you're human?"

"Your wit is sharp today, buddy."

Chuckling, Joseph said, "As for Jazelle, my family has begged her to move out to the ranch. Mom even told her they'd build her a little house a short distance from the big house. But she's very independent and full of pride. She doesn't want handouts of any kind."

Joseph's description of Jazelle didn't surprise Connor. He'd noticed the straight line of her shoulders and the proud tilt to her chin. No, he thought, she was hardly the sort to ask for handouts.

"What about Jazelle's parents? Guess she doesn't want to live around them, either?"

Joseph grunted. "I don't know much about them. Except that they divorced a long time ago and her father moved away. Her mother lives in Wickenburg. But from what Tessa tells me, the woman is a— Well, let's just say she's an unpleasant woman."

So other than the Hollisters, Jazelle didn't have much of a family unit around her. Connor had been in the same situation since he was teenager. "I get the fact that she wants to be on her own. That way she doesn't have to consider anybody but her and her little boy."

Joseph turned away from the computer screen long enough to shoot Connor a pointed look. "You would see it that way."

"Look, Joe, we don't all come from big families like you. It's different for people like me and Jazelle."

Joseph grimaced. "Tessa wants Jazelle to find a good man to marry. She has this romantic notion that everyone should have someone to love. I've tried to tell my wife that finding real love isn't always easy."

Connor wouldn't know about real love. He'd never hunted the elusive emotion. Why bother? Love, if there truly was such a thing, never lasted. It either burned itself to a pile of useless ashes or died a slow, painful death of boredom. And if that didn't happen, death usually stepped in to end things. No, Connor didn't need or want that kind of misery.

While Joseph turned his attention to back to the computer, Connor contemplated the idea of Jazelle falling in love and getting married. For some reason, his brain revolted against the image. She didn't need some creep hanging around, taking advantage of her soft heart. And that little boy of hers damned sure didn't need a jerk who didn't know the first thing about being a father.

Like you, Connor? Yeah, you have memories of your father and they're all good. But you were just a kid when he died. What you learned from him was not enough to prepare you for family life. No, the only thing you're good for is a laugh and a good time.

Frustrated with the annoying voice in his head, Connor rose from the desk and walked over to the open doorway. Outside in the wide corridor, deputies and other personnel were going to and fro, while a cacophony of ringing phones and voices overpowered the sound of the rattling air-conditioner vent above his head.

Turning away from the doorway, he watched Joseph continue to type at a slow, steady pace. "Are you writing a saga? I'm getting damned hungry. We haven't eaten in eight hours. And we're supposed to be back on the road in thirty minutes. We'll have to eat in the truck. Again."

"Patience, Deputy Murphy. I'm nearly there." Joseph tapped the last few words of the report then directed the information to its proper destination. "Okay. Finished."

Connor grabbed his hat from a hall tree and levered it onto this head. "Hallelujah! I'm finally going to get to eat."

Joseph put the computer on sleep mode and pushed back his chair. "Um, before we go, Connor, I have a favor to ask."

Connor frowned. "Since when did you ever have to ask me for a favor? Whatever it is, I'll do it."

"This isn't just any favor," Joseph warned. "I want you to come out to the ranch tomorrow night."

Normally on the Saturday nights he wasn't on duty, Connor drove out to the Fandango Club for drinks and dancing with the prettiest available women. It was his favorite way to blow off steam. But if Joseph needed him, he could forgo the Fandango this once.

"The ranch?" Connor asked. "You mean your ranch, the Bar X?"

Rising from the desk chair, Joseph shook his head. "When I say *the* ranch, I still mean Three Rivers. It's engrained in me."

Connor was a bit surprised. "What's going on that I need to be there?"

"I wish I could say we're having a party, but actually, it's a meeting with my brothers and Uncle Gil. We're going to discuss some of the options we have about finding Dad's killer."

Killer. Joseph had often talked to Connor about his dad's death, but he'd never used that particular word before. "Killer? Guess you've finally reached the point where you're going to call your father's death a murder. Aloud, I mean."

"I reached that point some time ago. I just don't go around saying the word in front of the women-folk of the family," he said then added with wry sarcasm, "As if that's going to spare them the pain of the incident."

About eight years ago, Joseph's father, Joel Hollister, had been found on the range, one boot stuck in the stirrup while the remainder of his body lay bloodied and mangled on the ground. No one knew exactly how far the ranch patriarch had been dragged across the rough terrain. Nor did they have any idea why the trusty steed would've bolted with his rider dangling from the saddle. During the years since, Joseph had worked tirelessly to gather clues to determine what had actually occurred to cause his father's untimely death.

"I'm happy to help. But your family might think I'm butting in on your private business," Connor pointed out.

Joseph frowned at him. "Wrong. They'll be happy to know you're working with me on this," he said. "And, if it will give you some incentive to make the trip out to the ranch, Reeva will be serving dinner to all of us."

Over the years, Joseph had often boasted about the Hollister family cook. And, though he'd never met the woman, he had eaten a few delicious meals that she'd prepared. But suddenly Connor wasn't thinking about feasting on a rich dinner. His mind had already leaped to the ranch's housekeeper.

What in heck is wrong with you, Connor? Jazelle has two-story house, white picket fence and a baby cradle written all over her! She's the last woman you need to be eyeing!

In spite of the sarcastic warning going off in his head, Connor said, "You can count me in, Joe."

Joseph settled his cowboy hat onto his head and nudged Connor toward the door. "Thanks, buddy. I'll be sure to tell Mom to have Jazelle set another plate on the table."

So that meant *she* would be there, Connor thought with a spurt of excitement. And suddenly he didn't give a damn about missing a night at the Fandango. He was going to see Jazelle again.

Chapter Three

"Jazelle, why don't you let Raine come upstairs and spend the evening with Andy and Abby while you help Reeva? Once dinner gets in full swing, you'll be too busy to keep a close eye on him, and the kids love to play together."

Jazelle looked away from the sink of dirty pots and pans over to Blake's wife. The tall brunette was as beautiful and slender as the day she'd married the manager of Three Rivers Ranch and was still just as kind and lovely on the inside, Jazelle thought.

"Oh, thanks for the offer, Kat," she said doubtfully. "But you already have your hands full with the twins. And, anyway, it's not your place to babysit my son."

Katherine swatted away that argument with a short laugh. "Why not? You babysit the twins every day. So don't argue. Little Joe and Spring are coming, too, so I'll let all the kids have a little picnic on the floor. They'll love it."

At the industrial-size cookstove, a tall, slender woman with a steel-gray braid hanging down her back, stirred a large pot of *carne guisada*. The seasoned meat had been simmering for hours and the delicious aroma now permeated the large kitchen located at the back of the big three-story ranch house.

"Better listen to her, Jazelle," Reeva said. "You know how it is when a bunch of men get together. Want, want and want some more. You'll be running your legs off."

Knowing from experience that Reeva was right, Jazelle gave in. "Okay, Kat. I'd be grateful if you'd take Raine upstairs with you. But if he starts giving you trouble, just call down here to the kitchen. I'll come after him."

Katherine shook her head. "No chance. If I can't corral three children at once, then I need some mothering lessons. Besides, Vivian and Sawyer are bringing Nick home this evening from the reservation. He and his cousin, Hannah, will help me with the kids."

Jazelle went back to washing a set of round cake pans. "Oh, good. I'll get to see the twins."

Vivian, the middle daughter of the Hollister siblings, had married fellow park ranger, Sawyer White-horse, a little more than two years ago. At that time

Vivian already had a thirteen year old daughter, Hannah, from a prior marriage. Since marrying Sawyer, Vivian had given birth to identical twin boys named Jacob and Johnny. With thick black hair and brown eyes, the one-year-old boys closely resembled their handsome Apache father. And because they'd both started walking at ten months, they were quite a handful.

"I hope someone has put up anything that isn't bolted down," Reeva said. "Otherwise, those two little rascals will have the place in shambles."

Laughing, Katherine said, "Roslyn is doing that right now and I'm going to go help her. The two of us will make sure everything is put away and out of reach of little hands."

Katherine departed the kitchen and Jazelle glanced at the large clock positioned above the breakfast booth. "As soon as I finish here, I'll go set the table," she told Reeva. "Do you know if Tessa and her kids are going to eat downstairs tonight?"

"No. She and the little ones are going upstairs. So are Vivian and the twins," Reeva answered. "And Nick and Hannah are going to eat here in the kitchen with me. Oh…and Emily-Ann is coming, but she's going upstairs with the other women. So that should mean you need nine place settings for the dining room."

"Nine?" Frowning, Jazelle began to count on her fingers. "I'm getting eight, Reeva."

The cook dumped a large can of hominy into a

saucepan and switched on the burner. "Oh, I forgot to mention that Joe's bringing a guest tonight. His partner. I think his name is Connor."

Jazelle felt like Reeva had just thrown a bucket of ice water in her face. She stood frozen in her tracks, her mind whirling. Connor Murphy was coming here tonight for dinner? She couldn't believe it. In all of the seven years she'd worked at Three Rivers, she'd never once seen the man in this house. But then she often had to run errands away from the ranch, she reasoned. Or he could've visited on her days off.

Hoping Reeva hadn't noticed her stunned reaction, Jazelle slowly dried her hands on a dish towel. "I, uh, wonder why he's coming to dinner."

Reeva didn't bother glancing in Jazelle direction. "No one has said anything that I've heard, but it's clear to me that the guys are planning to ramp up their investigation into Joel's death. I expect Joe believes another deputy would be a big help in the matter."

"The late Sheriff Maddox ruled the case an accident and closed it years ago," Jazelle mused out loud.

Reeva snorted. "Any person who believes Joel's death was an accident needs their head examined. Ray Maddox ruled it that way because he had no proof it was anything else. And as the sheriff of Yavapai County, he had to follow the rules."

Absently twisting the dish towel in her hands, Jazelle asked thoughtfully, "Joe and Connor can't work on the case now, can they? I mean with it being closed and all."

"Not while they're on duty. But they can on their own personal time."

"Oh. I see."

Jazelle tossed the towel onto the cabinet counter then walked over to a china hutch where a set of Maureen Hollister's better china was stored. Instead of opening the cabinet and pulling down the plates, she simply stood there staring into space.

Ever since Joseph and Connor had dropped by her house, she'd tried not to think about the blond-haired, blue-eyed deputy. But his sexy image had continued to pop randomly into her thoughts. These past few days, she'd been telling herself she'd never see the man again. She'd also been telling herself that never seeing him again was a good thing. He was a walking hunk of trouble. The sort she didn't need. Yet the mere thought of seeing him tonight was enough to make her heart leap into a rapid flutter.

"Maureen says everyone should probably be gathered in the family room by six o'clock, so you might be getting the drinks ready as soon as you get the dining room set," Reeva said. "I figure most will want margaritas, except for Holt."

"Yes, I know, Reeva. He'll want his bourbon and Coke over ice."

From across the room, Jazelle heard Reeva let out a tired sigh. She glanced over her shoulder to see the woman press a palm to her forehead.

Forgetting the dishes, Jazelle walked over to the cook and put an arm around her slender shoulders. Reeva was seventy-three but Jazelle never thought of her as being elderly or feeble. She had the energy and strength of a woman half her age and there was hardly a wrinkle to be found in her light brown complexion.

"Reeva, are you getting sick?"

The cook dropped her hand from her forehead. "No, honey. I'm fine—just a little weary—that's all."

"Go over to the table and sit for a minute or two," Jazelle ordered sternly. "I'll get you something cool to drink."

"We don't have time for that! And I'm not sick," she muttered crossly. "I really just want to curse a blue streak. That might make me feel better!"

Deciding Reeva wasn't experiencing some sort of medical episode, Jazelle took a step back and studied the disgusted expression on the woman's face. "What's wrong? Are you tiring of all these special dinners and parties Maureen has been having here lately?"

"Hell no!" Reeva grabbed up a pepper grinder and twisted several turns over the hominy. "I have to cook whether it's a special occasion or not. That's my job, and I like it or I wouldn't be doing it. I'm… sad and worried and mad, that's what. My granddaughter called me earlier this afternoon."

Reeva wasn't one to talk about her family—not that she had many relatives to talk about. She'd been a widow since her husband died in the Vietnam War more than forty years ago and had raised their daughter, Liz, all on her own. Unfortunately, Liz hadn't grown up to have the heart or morals of her mother. The woman had hated everything about her life in small-town Arizona and had moved to California, where she'd set out to climb the social ladder and find herself a rich husband.

Because Liz had been embarrassed to admit her mother was a house cook on a ranch, Liz told her friends that Reeva was a secretary for a law firm in Phoenix. Along this same deceptive path, Liz had found herself a rich husband and bore him a daughter. Predictably, the marriage hadn't lasted. Nor had any kind of meaningful relationship with Reeva. The two women hadn't spoken in years. However, the granddaughter was a different matter. Sophia called Reeva often, and had even made the trip from California to visit her grandmother on a few occasions.

"And?" Jazelle prodded Reeva to explain. "Is anything wrong?"

"Sophia had a miscarriage. She was nearly four months into the pregnancy. In my mind, I was already thinking of myself as great-grandmother. But it wasn't to be."

"Oh, Reeva," Jazelle said gently, "why didn't you say something earlier? You should've told Maureen you needed time off. I could've done the cooking. You've taught me plenty enough about preparing food to get by for a few meals."

"Listen, honey, you know what it's like to get bad news. You don't fall apart. Women like you and me just buck up and keep going."

There was plenty of truth to Reeva's words. She and Jazelle had both gone through tough times. But that hardly meant they didn't feel as much loss and pain as any other woman.

Jazelle frowned. "You don't have to be a piece of steel all the time, Reeva. You are human, after all. Not a robot. And the Hollisters aren't holding a whip over your head."

Reeva's dark eyes leveled a pointed look at Jazelle. "Other than Sophia, the Hollisters are the only family I have. And I think the same thing goes for you. We don't work here because it's easy, but because we're a part of something big. And we're loved." She turned back to the stove and pushed a wooden spoon through a pot of simmering Spanish rice. "I'll be all right, honey," she added, her voice gentling. "You go on and get things ready."

Time was ticking on and Jazelle still had a jillion things to do before dinner was served. Including changing out of her stained work shirt and jeans and into the cotton dress she'd brought to work with her.

Early this morning, she'd snatched the first thing she'd come to in her closet and tossed it into the back seat of her truck, along with a duffel filled with Raine's favorite toys. If she'd known then that Connor Murphy was coming to Three Rivers tonight, would she have tried to find something a bit more flattering to wear? Probably not. It would take far more than a nice dress to catch the deputy's attention. And even if she could get a second glance from him, she didn't want or need that kind of distraction in her life.

Holding on to that determined thought, Jazelle returned to the china hutch and quickly began to pull out the dishes. "I guess Sophia's fiancé was disappointed about the miscarriage. They're planning to be married soon, aren't they?"

The curse word Reeva muttered only came out of the woman's mouth whenever she was really aggravated.

"I should've already told you about that—he left about a month or so ago. Accused Sophia of intentionally getting pregnant after he'd told her he didn't want any kids. Said a kid would only hamper his chances to work his way into an executive position." She let out a contemptable snort. "I hope Liz is happy now. She's managed to drag Sophia down with all her so-called airs. Now, Sophia doesn't have the baby or the bastard who was supposed to love her."

Jazelle was trying to think of some sort of reply to Reeva's outburst when she heard the woman sniff. The heartbreaking sound brought tears to Jazelle's eyes. Reeva's gruff manner was only her way of covering up her pain and worries. In truth, the woman was as soft as a marshmallow and, next to Raine, Jazelle loved her as much or more than she'd ever loved anyone.

"Guess it was supposed to end this way, though," Reeva added.

Jazelle glanced over her shoulder to see the cook slapping homemade tortillas onto a grill. "Things happen for a reason, Reeva. And we have to believe it will all work out for the best."

She'd barely gotten the words out when the sound of footsteps announced a third person entering the kitchen. Jazelle glanced over to see Maureen, looking lovelier than usual in a blue shirtwaist dress that went all the way to her ankles. Her chestnut hair was swept into an elegant French twist, while turquoise-and-silver earrings dangled from her ears.

The Hollister matriarch must've sensed the tension in the air because she stopped abruptly in the middle of the room and looked from one woman to the other.

"What's wrong in here? It feels like a tomb."

"Nothing," Reeva said flatly. "We're just running a bit behind, that's all."

Maureen glanced questioningly over at Jazelle. "I noticed the dining table is empty," she remarked. "Do I need to help you two with anything?

Now wasn't the time to explain that Reeva was having a bit of an emotional meltdown. Maureen could hear about that later. "No! I'm headed there right now, Maureen." She grabbed up a stack of plates and hurried toward the swinging door that led into the dining room. "And I'll bring the drinks to the family room in just a few minutes."

* * *

Twenty minutes later, Connor was sitting in a leather armchair, gazing around the enormous den of the Three Rivers Ranch house. Each time Connor had actually been inside Joseph's family home, he'd been a bit awed by the sheer size and workmanship of the house.

With tall ceilings, tongue-and-groove walls painted soft, neutral colors, and planked cypress flooring, the house really couldn't be called lavish, but it was definitely beautiful and warm. Obviously, it had been built back in an era when most of the carpentry work had been painstakingly done with hand tools. A remarkable feat, considering the ornate corner moldings and wide beams supporting the ceilings.

The furniture was all leather, including two couches in dark burgundy and three stuffed armchairs in a warm, butterscotch color. Spotted cowhide rugs were scattered here and there across the rich patina of the floor, while enlarged photos of ranching scenes decorated the walls. A large fireplace stretched across one corner of the room, while a modest-size TV sat in the opposite corner.

With so many family members living in the same house, Connor doubted it was ever quite enough for anyone to watch a TV program without distractions. But Joseph had told him that his brothers and their families all had upstairs suites so everyone could have their privacy.

Connor had grown up in a two-bedroom shotgun house with gray asphalt siding and a tiny concrete square for a porch. He'd worn jeans purchased from a discount store and his boots hadn't been replaced until holes appeared in the bottoms of the soles. But as kids, he and Joseph had never considered the differences in their background as important. And now that they were grown men, they still didn't.

"Tag, I was beginning to think you weren't going to make it."

Connor turned his head in the direction of Chandler's voice to see a tall, dark-haired cowboy entering the room. The man took off his hat and placed it on a wall table near the open doorway before he reached to shake the veterinarian's hand.

"Sorry, I'm running a bit late," he said to Chandler. "About the time we were ready to leave the house, Emily-Ann had a bout of nausea."

"Oh, poor thing. Is there anything I can do? You know I'm good with doctoring horses, but I'm even better with pregnant women. Just ask Roslyn," Chandler joked.

The other man laughed. "Thanks for the offer, Doc, but she's feeling a bit better now. She's gone upstairs to be with the rest of the girls."

By now Joseph had risen from his seat on the couch and motioned for the two men to join him. "Come here, Tag," he called out. "I want you to meet someone."

Connor left the chair and walked over to the three

men, where Joseph proceeded to introduce him to the tall cowboy.

"This is Taggart O'Brien, our new ranch foreman. He's been with us a few months now. Ever since Matthew married my sister, Camille, and moved to Red Bluff," Joseph said then pointed his thumb toward Connor. "And, Tag, this is Connor Murphy. He's been a Yavapai deputy sheriff for as long as I have. And a good friend since we were kids."

"Which is a hell of a long time," Connor said with a laugh. He reached to shake hands with the man. "Nice to meet you, Taggart. So you're the Texan who took Matthew's place. I've heard lots of good things about you from Joe."

Taggart chuckled. "Nobody could take Matthew's place, but I'm doing my best. And just call me Tag— everybody does."

Voices suddenly sounded behind them and Chandler glanced over his shoulder. "Here comes Jazelle," he announced. "If Holt doesn't keep her cornered, we'll finally get something to drink."

The group of men parted just enough to give Connor a view of the housekeeper pushing a cart loaded with glasses and bottles over to a wet bar that stretched across a far corner of the room. This evening she was wearing a dress that wrapped across the front of her body and tied at the waist. The fabric was a gold and bronze pattern; the colors making the blond hair coiled in a knot atop her head appear to be an even richer shade of honey.

Knowing he was staring, but unable to tear his gaze away from the young beauty, he watched her park the cart then hand Holt a squatty glass filled with dark liquid. The horseman grinned and gave her shoulders a one-armed squeeze. How would that feel, Connor wondered, to be that close to her? He'd definitely like to find out.

While he was fantasizing, Joseph nudged his shoulder forward. "Let's go see what Jazelle has to offer. I can promise you she makes a mean margarita. But if you'd prefer gin instead of tequila, she makes a delicious Salty Dog."

Mentally shaking himself, Connor said, "You know me, Joe. I'm not picky when it comes to alcohol."

"I've hardly forgotten the fact," Joseph joked. "Put a glass of anything eighty proof in your hand and a woman hanging on your arm and you're a contented fellow."

Connor had heard this kind of teasing from Joseph for years and he'd always laughed it away. But for some reason tonight, he didn't much feel like laughing. In fact, Connor didn't much appreciate being thought of as a womanizer.

What the hell was wrong with him? He *was* a womanizer. And at this point in his life, he was far too old to start changing his ways.

With that determined thought, Connor followed Joseph across the room to where Jazelle was handing out drinks to Chandler and Blake. Once the two brothers drifted away from the bar, she looked around and her brown eyes instantly collided with Connor's. The contact was a jolt to his senses.

"Hello, Jazelle," he said.

Connor watched her lips part, her brows arch slightly beneath the wisp of hair falling onto her forehead. Now that he was standing only an arm's-length away, he could see that she'd darkened her lashes and dabbed a bit of cherry color on her lips. But that was the only bit of makeup he could detect. Not that she needed it. Her skin was dewy and flawless.

Her cheeks flushed with a pretty pink color. "Hello, Connor, Joe. What would you two guys like to drink?" she asked.

"I couldn't miss one of your margaritas," Joseph said with a grin. "You know how I like mine."

"Right. No salt, with a lime wedge," she said.

As Jazelle deftly put the drink together, Connor's gaze swept over her lovely face. Her smooth skin had him thinking of a piece of caramel candy. The soft kind that melted sweet and delicious on his tongue. And those berry-colored lips—somehow he knew they would taste even better than they looked.

"What would you like, Connor? You don't have to drink a margarita. I have all sorts of other choices." She made a sweeping gesture with her hand over the bottles and glasses lined up on the wet bar.

She could serve him a glass of half-soured milk and, in his muddled state of mind, he'd think it was perfect. "Uh, just fix something you think suits me," he told her.

Her brown eyes slid over his face and Connor felt a slow burn spread through the pit of his stomach.

"You might not like it," she warned.

"Don't worry about that, Jazelle," Joseph told her. "As long as it gives him a buzz, he'll be happy."

The corners of her lips tilted slightly upward and Connor tried to remember if he'd ever seen a sexier sight. "Don't listen to Joe. He'll have you thinking all kinds of bad things about me."

Joseph laughed. "I expect Jazelle has already been thinking a bunch of bad things about you and she'd be right about every one of them."

Connor frowned at him. "Aw, now, Joe, give me a break. I haven't been to a Hollister dinner in long time. Be nice to me."

Chuckling again, Joseph playfully swatted his shoulder. "I'm just kidding. You stay here and get your drink. I'm going to go talk with Tag."

Joseph walked away and Connor tried not to notice that he and Jazelle were the only two people in this far corner of the room. Otherwise, he might not be able to manage to utter one sensible word.

The idea was hilarious. Since when had he ever been tongue-tied around a woman? Not ever. But he was feeling damned close to it now.

"So what do you think about the ranch house?" she asked as she poured some sort of pink liquid into a metal shaker.

"It's huge and impressive. The workmanship is a marvel. Especially when you consider it was built in the 1860s. Sort of makes me feel like I've stepped back in time."

"The house is full of history. Just like the ranch." She added lime juice and sugar to the pink stuff, stirred it and then poured in a hefty amount of tequila. "Except for adding the bathrooms and indoor plumbing, everything has been maintained just as it was built."

Mesmerized by the graceful movement of her hands, Connor watched her edge the rim of a glass with lime juice then dip it in coarse salt. With that done, she flipped the glass over, filled it with ice then poured in the whole concoction. After she threw in a lime wedge, she offered him the frosty glass.

"Here it is," she said. "And don't be bashful. Tell me if you rather toss it in the trash can."

Him bashful? Good thing Joseph hadn't heard her remark, Connor thought. He'd be laughing himself silly.

Grinning, Connor took the glass. "I'm afraid I'm just a plain ole beer kind of guy, Jazelle. You'll have to tell me what this is."

She smiled at him and Connor felt like a kid who'd just been handed an unexpected Christmas gift. What was it about this woman? Her smile was like an iridescent light circling him with warmth.

"It's a Paloma," she told him. "Are you going to try it? Or just hold it?"

He sipped the drink then purposely cast her a bland look. "It's okay."

Her expression turned to a mixture of disappointment and disbelief. "Really? Just okay?"

He chuckled. "Sorry. I just had to tease you a bit. Actually, it's delicious. Thank you for going to the trouble of making it."

"That's my job."

She was politely saying she hadn't done anything special for him. But Connor wanted to think otherwise.

"Where did you learn bartending skills?" he asked.

A faint smile touched her lips. "Not in a bar, if that's what you're thinking."

"I wasn't thinking anything of the sort. You don't look like the bar type," he said and felt a wave of heat wash up his neck. "Uh, not that I'm acquainted with the type—all that much."

The smile on her face deepened enough to cause a dimple to appear in her cheek and Connor decided he'd never seen a more enchanting woman. Or had one make him feel so downright goofy.

"No," she said slyly. "I'm sure you rarely see the inside of a bar."

He took a long sip of his drink and realized the pink liquid she'd put in it was grapefruit soda. He'd never really cared for the stuff, but the sugar softened the tartness and the tequila was already working on his senses. Or was she the one that was tilting his faculties? Either way, Connor knew he needed to leave the housekeeper's company and go join the menfolk. But he didn't want to. Not yet.

"Wrong. I couldn't count the times Joe and I have been called to break up bar fights."

"That sounds like a hazardous job."

He supposed it would sound dangerous to her. To Connor, it wasn't nearly as bad as vehicle crashes or domestic violence calls. "Well, when you have intoxicated people going at each other with fists and knives or guns, anything can happen. But most of the time we make arrests without incident. Just another day at the office, so to speak."

Her brown eyes were regarding him closely and Connor wondered what she was thinking. That she didn't like lawmen? Or just didn't like him?

What Jazelle is thinking about you hardly matters, Connor. From what Joseph says, she doesn't want any man in her life. And you'd be asking for trouble to think you might change her mind.

She said, "Well, I learned how to mix drinks from Reeva. She's the cook here at Three Rivers. Years ago, when she was very young, she worked in a bar and grill. That's where she learned and now she's taught me. Not that I ever plan to work as a bartender." She shrugged and gave him a half smile. "But a person never knows what he or she might have to do to survive."

Connor realized he wanted to ask her all sorts of things. He wanted to know all about her wants and wishes. Not just for now, but far into the future. Where did she want to be five or ten years from now? Still here on the ranch or married to some man who would take her far away from the Arizona desert?

"I don't think you need to worry about your job security," he said, thinking she must've served him some kind of magical potion. He'd never been interested in a woman's personal history or, for that matter, her future plans.

She suddenly cleared her throat and fastened the lid tightly over the ice bucket. "I might if I don't get back to the kitchen. Please excuse me."

Connor watched her leave the den before he slowly walked back over to where the other men had taken various seats on the leather furniture.

Joseph gestured to an empty space next to him on the long couch. "Mom says dinner is running a tad late, and Vivian and Sawyer haven't gotten here yet, so you might as well get comfortable while we wait."

With his glass in hand, Connor carefully eased down onto the couch. "I heard Tag say his wife upstairs. Where are Tessa and the kids? Didn't they come with you?"

"Except for Mom, the women of the family decided to eat upstairs with the kids."

"Sounds like they don't like you men's company," Connor joked.

Joseph chuckled. "Think about it, Connor. There are two sets of twins, my two babies and Chandler's two. Plus two teenagers—Nick and Hannah. With ten kids around the dining table, I doubt we could hear ourselves think, much less talk."

Connor shook his head. "Why anyone would want to be a parent is beyond me."

"One of these days, you'll figure it out," Joseph told him then gestured toward the glass in Connor's hand. "What did Jazelle make for you?"

"A Paloma. I'd never heard of one, but it's very good."

One of Joseph's brows took on a clever arch. "Wow. She only makes those for special guests. Like cattle or horse buyers. You must rank up there with the VIPs."

"Not hardly. Since I'm rarely out here for dinner, I think she wants me to be impressed with —the Hollister hospitality."

Joseph rolled his eyes with disbelief. "Oh, is that it? Well, enjoy your Paloma. Maybe you can talk her into making you another."

Connor chuckled. "I'm not even going to try."

But before the night was over, he was going to do his damnedest to talk to her again.

Chapter Four

"You were right, Reeva. Each time I've taken something to the dinner table, the men have been talking about Joel's death and something about the auction barn at Phoenix," Jazelle said as she gathered dessert plates from the china hutch. "I wonder what that's about—the Phoenix part, I mean."

"I'm only guessing, but Joel went down there on a regular basis. He liked to watch the cattle sell and sometimes he'd buy a few cows or steers. Mostly to put down on Red Bluff. Maybe they're thinking Joel had trouble with someone at the sale barn. Maureen doesn't talk that much about it to me. And I'm not going to ask her. She'll tell us when she's ready."

Reeva glanced over her shoulder at Jazelle. "Did you whip up the whipping cream for the cobbler?"

"Yes. It's already chilled," Jazelle told her as she placed the dishes on a rolling cart alongside a pan of apple cobbler and a large glass bowl layered with strawberry shortcake. "After I serve everyone at the dining table, I'll take dessert upstairs. I need to check on Raine to make sure he's not causing problems. And I want to see Johnny and Jacob."

She pushed the loaded cart out of the kitchen and entered the dining room just as Gil was saying, "I've made at least five trips there in the past six weeks and I've not made any headway. Most of the employees have changed since Joel attended the auctions. A few vaguely remembered him, but none recalled seeing him with a woman."

The last part of Gil's remark caught Jazelle by surprise. Joel with a woman? What could that be about? The man had supposedly been the epitome of a family man.

As Jazelle made her way to the end of the table where Maureen was seated, the Hollister matriarch was saying, "There has to be a way of figuring out who she was. Joel used to be friends with a rancher from down around Cave Creek and they often met up at the sale barn. He might remember the woman or know of her."

"That was Ben Grady, Mom." Blake spoke up. "We've already thought of him. I tried calling him, but his wife informed me that he'd passed away last year."

"Oh. That's sad news. In more ways than one," she said. Realizing that Jazelle was standing near her shoulder, she looked up. "Oh, Jazelle, you have dessert?"

The woman certainly didn't appear to be distressed over the idea of Joel being linked to a woman, Jazelle thought. But the connection could've been anything other than a romantic one. And besides, Maureen was definitely growing very close to Gil, who was Joel's older brother. Could be the retired detective was taking away all the grief and pain she'd endured over her husband's death.

Jazelle nodded. "Take your pick. Apple cobbler or strawberry shortcake."

Maureen said, "I'd prefer the cobbler, but the shortcake has less calories. At least that's what Reeva tells me, so give me a small dish of it."

Holt, the third Hollister brother and fourth sibling of the family, was quick to tease. "Mom, if you'd help me all day in the horse pen, you wouldn't have to worry about extra calories."

"Ha! I spend plenty of hours in the saddle," she retorted and then grinned and winked at Gil, who was sitting kitty-corner from her. "Not falling out of it like you, Holt."

Everyone laughed while Holt groaned loudly. "Mom, you're getting mean in your older years. Especially to me, when you know I've always been your favorite son."

"Favorite or troublesome?"

Grinning, Holt looked up at Jazelle. "Tell them, Jazelle. I'm *your* favorite Hollister brother, aren't I?"

She gave him an indulgent smile. "Always, Holt. That's why I hide the bourbon bottle from you."

Wailing loudly, he plopped his fork down on the table. "Not you, too, Jazelle. You've cut my heart to pieces."

She handed the dessert to Maureen. "I'm only teasing, Holt. You know that. Of course you're my favorite."

The teasing banter didn't let up as Jazelle continued to move on down the long table. However, by the time she reached Connor, the subject had changed to Chandler, who was taking a roasting for having the reputation of always being late.

Chandler defended himself. "Tag tells me that doctors are supposed to be late."

Sawyer chuckled. "Roslyn says you were very nearly late to your own wedding."

"That's because one of Holt's overdue mares had to have a C-section. I couldn't leave her just because the preacher was getting impatient."

"Not to mention Roslyn," Holt joked.

While more laughter sounded around the table, Jazelle looked down and locked gazes with Connor. "Would you like dessert?" she asked, trying to ignore the crazy flutter in the pit of her stomach.

"Thanks, I'd like the cobbler. I'm like Holt—I'm not worried about the calories."

The man was all lean muscle and she doubted he had to work himself up into a lather at a gym to keep his fit physique. No, he looked like a natural to her.

"You're a lucky man."

The corners of his lips tilted upward. "Are you going to have dessert?"

"After I have my dinner."

"You've not eaten yet?"

Doing her best to avoid eye contact with the man, she said, "I don't eat until everyone else is finished. It's the way of my job."

She ladled a hefty amount of cobbler onto the small plate and dolloped several spoons of whipping cream over the top. As she leaned across his right arm to place the dessert in front of him, she caught the faint scent of sage and spices. The masculine mixture suited him perfectly, she thought. As did the gray shirt that molded to his broad shoulders and made his sky-blue eyes appear even more vivid.

At that moment, those eyes looked up at her and Jazelle let out a long, silent sigh. She could only hope that Connor Murphy wasn't invited to any more Hollister dinners. Otherwise, she was going to suffer a mental breakdown.

"Thank you," he murmured.

Somewhere in the depths of his eyes she spotted a gleam that sent a finger of heat trailing down her spine. Was he honestly trying to flirt with her? No.

The guy probably had more girlfriends than he knew what to do with. He didn't need the attention of a single mom who was so overworked she was too exhausted to dream about romance, much less have one.

"You're welcome," she said then hurriedly moved on down the table before anyone noticed she was lingering at Connor's chair.

Much later, after coffee had been served in the den and the conversation had turned to subjects other than the investigation of Joel's death, Connor excused himself from the group and went in search of a restroom.

He'd just left the facilities and was headed back down a hallway toward the den when Jazelle, carrying a huge tray, stepped through a door. As she walked toward him, Connor went to meet her.

"That's far too heavy for you to carry," he told her as he noted the tray laden with desserts. "Let me help you."

"That isn't necessary. I do this all the time."

She started to step around him but Connor wasn't about to let her get away that easily.

"Maybe you do, but you don't have to while I'm here to help. Where are you taking it?"

"Upstairs to the women and kids."

He pulled the tray from her grasp. "I'll carry it. Just show me the way."

"Really, Connor, I'm not a weakling. You should go back to the den—with the men."

She was clearly trying to get rid of him, but Connor didn't let it put him off. In fact, he decided he rather liked the challenge.

"The men aren't missing me. They're talking cattle and horses. And I don't know much about either."

She cocked a brow at him. "What do you know about? Collaring crooks and breaking up bar fights?"

He grinned. "Someone has to do it. And I'm fairly good at it. Just ask Joe."

She seemed unimpressed, but that shouldn't come as a surprise. She was used to being around the Hollister men. Compared to them, Connor was just a regular guy with a modest amount of money and skills.

"I'm sure you are," she said and then gestured down the hallway. "Well, if you think you have to help, then we'll go in this direction. About a third of the way down the hall, we'll turn left and take the stairs," she told him.

"I passed the staircase earlier when I was headed to the bathroom," he told her as they began to walk down the wide corridor. "This house has three floors, doesn't it?"

"That's right. We're going to the third. I think that's where everyone is gathered."

"You couldn't possibly clean this house by yourself. Do you?" he asked as they strolled onward. "You'd never have time to do anything else."

"Katherine and Roslyn both help, especially with laundry and things of that nature. And on certain days, another lady comes in to do some of the deeper cleaning. The kitchen requires the most work," she admitted. "Here on the ranch there's no such thing as light meals like toast for breakfast or sandwiches for supper. Maureen expects full meals to be served. Reeva also makes pastries for Blake's and Holt's offices at the barns. I usually take those down to the ranch yard about six in the morning, or earlier if they're expecting buyers."

They had reached the stairs and, as they began the climb side by side, Connor was acutely aware of her nearness. She smelled like some sort of flower that acted on his senses like an aphrodisiac. And, though she'd probably already taken thousands of steps today, she moved with a sensuality that took his thoughts on a slow, erotic journey.

Drawing in a deep breath, he tried to focus on their conversation. "Sounds like a lot of work to me. Do you enjoy it?"

She looked over at him and Connor could detect a bit of surprise on her face. What was that about? he wondered. Hadn't a man ever asked her about her job or whether she liked it?

"A long time ago, before Raine was born, I used to think I wanted to do something else. But that got put aside. Now I can't imagine being away from the ranch. You see, it's home to me. More than the home you visited the night of the Wallaces' break-in."

"Why do you feel that way? Because that house is a rental?"

She laughed so enthusiastically that Connor actually felt uncomfortable. What was so funny? He'd thought his question was perfectly normal.

"Oh, Connor, don't you know?" she asked. Spotting the frown on his face, her expression sobered. "Renting—owning—has nothing to do with it. Here, I'm surrounded by people who love me. That's what makes a home."

He stifled a groan. Every word that came out of her mouth reminded him that she was exactly the sort of woman he didn't need or want in his life. He wasn't about hearth or home or giving his devotion to only one woman. Being that hobbled would be akin to torture. And yet being in her company was rapidly becoming addictive to him.

After a moment, he said, "I understand."

"Really? You don't look as though you understand."

He tried not to sound annoyed. "Well, Jazelle, people like me live alone. We're surrounded by four walls and quietness. We don't know about loving and sharing and that sort of…thing."

Her brown eyes were suddenly full of somber shadows. "I'm sorry."

For him? Hell, no woman needed to feel sorry for him. He had everything he'd ever wanted. He was a contented man.

Look, Connor, you've stepped into unchartered territory. You wouldn't know the first thing about having a normal conversation with a real woman.

The women you date never talk about love and, if they did, it wouldn't be the kind that comes from the heart. They don't care that your insides are coarser than grit sandpaper. All they want is a good time. You get what you sow.

Connor was shoving at the self-deprecating voice in his head when they reached the second-floor landing.

"One more to go," Jazelle told him. "If you'd rather head back to the den, I can take the tray for the rest of the way."

Frowning now, he said, "I'd rather not."

"Stubborn, aren't you? How do you and Joe manage to get along?"

He chuckled. "We lock horns sometimes. But he's even more stubborn than me, so he usually wins out."

She asked, "Have you and Joe worked together for very long?"

"A little more than ten years. But we've been good friends since we were little boys. We're the same age, same classes all through school. Except that Joe was always the good guy and I was the rounder."

She slanted him a wry look "Was? Has that changed?"

To his surprise, he felt a rush of heat climb up his neck and onto his jawline. Man, what was that about? he wondered. He didn't think he knew how to blush.

"Well, I'm a fairly steady, dependable guy," he said. "At least, the Yavapai County Sheriff thinks so."

"I guess his opinion is the only one that matters."

Besides the sheriff and the rest of his peers at work, Connor normally didn't give a damn what other people thought of him. His work was his life and, outside of it, not much else mattered. Or at least, that's how he'd always felt about things until tonight. Until Jazelle's brown eyes had cast him a few censuring looks.

"Not the only one," he replied. "But it's up there at the top."

They finally reached the third landing and Jazelle pointed to a door on the left not more than ten feet away. "That's where we're going. The journey is over."

"I've gone this far. I might as well finish the trip," he told her.

She followed him over to the door. As he stood to one side with the tray, she rapped on the wooden panel with her knuckles.

"I hear plenty of crying and squealing inside," Connor said. "Maybe you should put in some earplugs before you go in there."

She gave him a faint smile. "I'm a mother. I'm used to it."

The door suddenly swung open and Joseph's sister stared at him with comical confusion. "Well, hello, Connor. When did deputies start doing waiter work?"

Glancing to his left, he noticed Jazelle was curiously watching their exchange. As though she was interested to see how the eldest sister of the Hollister group regarded him.

He let out an awkward chuckle. "Hi, Vivian. It's been a long time since I've seen you."

"Not since my wedding to Sawyer. It's nice to have you here at Three Rivers," she said then peered at the containers of desserts, a stack of paper bowls and plastic spoons. "You've brought our dessert, I see."

"I thought the tray was too heavy for Jazelle to carry all the way up here. So I offered to do it for her."

Her brows arching slightly, Vivian encompassed both him and Jazelle with a clever smile. "How sweet of you." She opened the door wider. "Come on in. I'll show you where to put the goodies."

Connor hadn't planned to go any further than the door, but to stop now would make him look pretty silly, so he followed the redhead into a fairly large sitting area.

Everywhere he looked, there were children and all of them seemed to be making noises at a high decibel. Laughing and shrieking, or crying and yelling, they were all trying to communicate with their little friends or trying to catch the attention of their mothers. Among the chaos, he recognized Raine and Little Joe, along with his younger sister Spring, sitting on the floor playing with a pile of building blocks. Nearby, a pair of black-haired twins were climbing on and off a couch. Those were Vivian and Sawyer's boys, he decided. They looked just like their father. Across the room, three more babies were on a padded pallet, two were waving their arms and bellowing in protest, while another was trying to crawl away.

"You can put the tray here, Connor," Vivian instructed as the two of them reached a tall table positioned along the far wall of the room.

He placed his load on the table and she gestured to the food. "It's a bit noisy in here, Connor, but you're welcome to join us."

"Thanks, but I've already had mine," he told her. "I'll just head back downstairs."

At that moment, Joseph's wife, Tessa, walked up behind him. "You're not going to get away that easily. You haven't said hello to the kids. In fact, I don't think you've ever seen Holt's son or Chandler's two babies."

Not giving him a chance to escape, Tessa took him by the arm and began to lead him away from Vivian.

"Tessa, I'm not good with kids and Joe doesn't know where I am. He'll be hunting me and—"

"Nonsense," she interrupted. "Joe knows you're a big boy who can find his way home."

Find his way home. According to Jazelle, he didn't have a home. Not the kind she wanted.

The thought had him glancing around to see if she'd followed him into the room and immediately spotted her over by the couch with a Whitehorse twin gathered up in each arm. The twins were apparently familiar with the housekeeper. They were both giggling and making an issue of patting her face, which was making her laugh in return.

Noticing he was gazing at Jazelle and the toddler-size twins, Tessa remarked, "She's wonderful with the kids. We'd all be lost if she wasn't around to help with them."

"Those two certainly seem to like her," Connor said, wondering how he'd managed to get himself boxed into a room with several women and a bunch of raucous children. All he'd wanted from this trip upstairs was a few minutes alone with Jazelle, not to take part in Babies 101.

"She has a way about her," Tessa replied.

That was an understatement, he thought. That special way of Jazelle's had taken such a hold on Connor that he was considering breaking his steadfast rule of never dating a woman with a child.

Trying to push that weak-willed urge aside, he followed Tessa over to the pallet where two babies were playing with an assortment of bright-colored toys. Only one of them bothered to look up. A boy with brown hair and greenish blue eyes.

"That must be Holt's son," Connor commented. "He has his dad's dimples."

Tessa laughed. "And his charm. Carter doesn't cry to get what he wants. He grins and goos. And the darker-haired boy is Billy, Chandler's son. He's just the opposite of his cousin. He screams to get attention, especially now that he's teething."

"Chandler should invest in some good soundproof earphones. He'd never hear the crying or screaming."

Tessa slanted him a droll look. "Connor, you're

deplorable. A parent doesn't want to tune out their child. Not a good parent, that is."

He let out an amused grunt. "Just goes to show you which kind of parent I'd be."

Rolling her eyes, she was about to give him some sort of retort when Connor felt something tugging on the back leg of his jeans.

Turning, he discovered Jazelle's son standing directly behind him. The boy's head was craned back as he stared curiously up at Connor.

"Hello, young man," Connor said.

The child tilted his head to a thoughtful angle. "You came to our house. With Uncle Joe."

Surprised that the child had remembered the brief incident, Connor squatted on his heels to be on the boy's level.

"That was me," he said. "My name is Connor and yours is Raine. Right?"

The blond-haired, blue-eyed boy gave him a slow nod. "You had a badge. Right there." He reached out and poked a finger against the pocket on the left side of Connor's shirt. Like a fist landing on his chin, the child's gentle touch caught him totally off guard.

"That's right," he said after a moment. "I'm a deputy sheriff. Like Joe."

"Oh. Why don't you have your badge on tonight? Did you stop being a deputy?"

The solemn look on the boy's face was enough to temper Connor's urge to chuckle. "I'm still a deputy. I'm just resting tonight, so I left my badge at home."

"Where is that?"

"You mean where do I live?"

Raine nodded.

Connor said, "I live up by Wilhoit. Have you ever been there?"

The child shook his head. "I go to town with Mommy. And we come here to the ranch. That's where we go."

In other words, Jazelle and Raine didn't get out of the circle of home and work. That didn't surprise him. But it made Connor realize that she and her son lived a narrow life. Although, he expected Jazelle would be the first to argue that point. He figured she didn't measure wealth by money in the bank or the scope of her life by the miles she traveled.

Connor was contemplating that notion when Raine suddenly spoke again.

"I used to go to kindergarten," he said. "But I don't do that anymore. I'm going to be in first grade now. Mommy says when I go back to school, I'll learn how to read. But I already know how. I can read my name and lots of other words."

"Wow! You must be a really smart boy."

Connor thought that might bring a smile to the boy's face, but so far he'd not seen anything close to one.

"Mommy says I'm smart. But Grandma says I'm mean."

Connor glanced up to Tessa for help, but she'd

already moved away to console her crying nephew, Billy.

"Uh, why would your grandma say something like that?" Connor asked Raine. "Do you do naughty things?"

"I broke her plate—but that was by accident. And I made the can opener quit working 'cause I was trying to open a can of tuna to give to the neighbor's cat. She says only mean boys get into stuff they're not supposed to do."

Sounded like this grandma had the same mindset his uncles had used on him as a child. To this day, Connor still remembered the hurtful things they'd said to him.

"Sometimes a guy just can't help it—things just happen. And if your grandma tells you that you're mean, just don't listen to her. You and me know better, don't we?" he said, giving the boy an encouraging smile.

Raine nodded enthusiastically. Then, without warning, he flung his arms around Connor's neck and squeezed tightly. "'Bye," he said as he finished the unexpected hug. "I gotta go play with Little Joe now."

The child raced across the room to where Little Joe and Spring were stacking building blocks into a square. Connor straightened to his full height and stood there watching the children until his gaze moved beyond them to Jazelle and the twins.

She set both of the toddlers back on the floor

and planted a kiss on each of their heads before she straightened away from the children and looked in his direction. Their gazes locked and Connor felt a hard jolt to his senses as she walked toward him.

Had she spotted him talking with her son? He'd not sought out the little boy. It had been the other way around. Still, he didn't want her to get the idea that he'd ever use the boy to make a good impression on her.

Once Jazelle reached him, she said, "I need to get back downstairs. Are you ready to leave?"

Did she have to ask? "Billy is getting madder by the minute," he said with a chuckle. "I think I'll spare my ears and go with you."

The two left the room and were near the second-floor landing when Connor finally found the nerve to reach for her arm and pull her aside.

"What are you doing?" she asked, glancing pointedly at the hand he'd wrapped around her upper arm.

"I wanted to speak with you a moment. Alone. Without the kids upstairs or the men downstairs."

An impatient frown creased her forehead and it dawned on Connor that she was vexed because he was keeping her from her work, not because she feared he was going to make a pass at her. Was he losing his masculine charm or what? he wondered.

Sighing heavily, she said, "Connor, I've already wasted too much time upstairs. The men are probably wanting more drinks and if Reeva has to leave the kitchen to take care of them, I'm going to feel awful."

"Just give me a minute," he pleaded. "That's all I ask."

Pressing her lips together, she stood, staring at him, waiting. "Your sixty seconds is ticking away," she reminded him.

Connor suddenly felt like a complete idiot. This wasn't what he should be doing, he scolded himself. He should be running down the stairs and out the front door. He should be putting this woman far, far out of his mind. Instead, he wanted to reach for her. He wanted to hold her next to him and feel her softness. He wanted to stroke her hair and breathe in the womanly scent of her skin.

"I, uh, wanted to ask you something personal."

The furrow between her brows deepened. "Personal? Really, Connor, I don't think—"

"I'm sorry," he interrupted. "I'm not doing this very well. But since you're in a hurry, I'll just blurt it out. Would you like to go out to dinner with me? Sometime soon. Maybe a couple of nights from now?"

Her mouth fell open and then, to Connor's amazement, she laughed. "Are you asking me out on a date?"

The Paloma she'd mixed for him must've done a number on his mouth, he decided. It felt like he'd been eating sand and had washed it down with a few cotton balls. "A date. Yes," he finally managed to say. "That's exactly what I'm asking."

Biting down on her bottom lip, she glanced away from him. "Then I'll have to say no."

Connor realized his hand was still on her arm and, considering her negative response, he should release his hold. But he didn't want to quit touching her, any more than he wanted to accept her refusal.

"Why?" he asked. "Is there something about me that you don't like?"

"I don't really know you."

"That's what dates are for, aren't they?" he asked. "For two people to get to know each other better."

Her somber gaze returned to his face. "I don't date. I don't even want to date. You're wasting your time."

The flat, disillusioned sound of her voice was like nothing Connor had encountered in a woman before. For that matter, he couldn't remember the last time any woman had turned down an invitation from him.

Well, you've been turned down now, Mr. Swagger. So go lick your wounded ego and get over it. This woman isn't your style. You need to call the redhead and forget you ever laid eyes on this one.

"Well, if that's the case, then we don't have to call it a date. It can be an outing—just to eat and talk."

Connor could see the wheels behind her brown eyes begin to spin. No doubt she was trying to figure out his motive. Well, good luck with that, he thought. Maybe if she came up with the answer, she'd share it with him. Because he sure as hell didn't know why he was bothering with a woman who was eyeing him like she expected him to hair over and grow fangs at any given moment.

"Thanks. But like I said, I don't date. And, anyway, I have to be away from Raine so much that I don't want to leave him with a sitter unless it's absolutely necessary."

Connor's first inclination was to argue that she deserved a bit of enjoyable time for herself. Then, out of nowhere, Raine's little face stared up at him.

Before Connor realized what he was about to do, he said, "If that's a problem, then you can bring Raine with you. We'll do something a little boy will enjoy."

Her expression turned skeptical. "How would you know what little boys enjoy?"

He slanted her a wry smile. "Probably because I happened to be one once—a long time ago."

Pink color seeped to the surface of her cheeks. "Sorry. I wasn't thinking."

"Yes, you were thinking—that I'm not a father. That I couldn't possibly know about such things. Right?"

She gave him a sheepish smile. "I guess you had to be Raine's age once."

"Once." He smiled, while wondering if that loud noise in his ears was the nervous drumbeat of his heart. "So what do you say? Is it a go?"

She released another long, heavy breath but, at the same time, her brown eyes appeared to soften.

"You really wouldn't mind Raine coming along?"

The disbelief in her voice made Connor feel worse than a heel. Admittedly, the kid was cute and he didn't have a thing against the boy, but in all honesty, he'd only made the offer to persuade Jazelle to go out with him. Well, that reason and the lost look in the boy's eyes. Connor had seen those same wary shadows whenever he'd looked at himself in the mirror and wondered why his own mother hadn't wanted him.

"I really don't mind," he told her.

She studied him for so long that he was finding it damned hard not to squirm.

Finally she said, "Okay. We'll go."

He'd never imagined that three simple little words could make him so happy. "Great! I'll call you tomorrow and we'll figure out the time and place."

"Fine," she said. "Now, would you please let me get back to work?"

"Of course." Connor guided her over to the staircase and as they descended the steps together, he wondered if he'd just won the lottery or paddled his canoe straight into a stretch of white-water rapids.

Chapter Five

A little over a week later, on Sunday afternoon, Jazelle wheeled her old truck to a halt at the side of the house and plucked up her handbag and leather-bound Bible lying on the seat next to her.

She glanced over at Raine, who was pushing mightily against the release button on the seat belt latch. "Do you need help with that?"

"Nope. I can do it." The belt popped loose and Raine climbed out of the booster seat. "Mommy, can we go to the ranch today? Nick would take me to the horse barn and let me ride Victor. Can we?"

"Not today. We have something else to do."

"Yeah, we have to eat," he announced with great fervor. "We always eat something good after church."

Jazelle looked at her son's eager face and wondered for the umpteenth time what she was doing. Why had she ever agreed to go out with Connor in the first place? Even if he'd said they wouldn't call it a date, it was still an outing with a man. And Raine wouldn't understand why they were spending time with a person they'd only met a few days ago.

Frankly, Jazelle didn't understand it herself. True, Connor was smoking hot to look at, but he wasn't her type. There wasn't any man on earth that was her type. Not after Spence's betrayal.

Pushing that dire thought aside, she said, "We're going to do something different today. So hurry up. Let's go in the house and I'll tell you about it."

Once they were out of the truck, Raine raced to the back porch and waited for Jazelle to unlock the door.

"Mommy, can we go eat at the Broken Spur?"

She pushed the door wide and nudged Raine inside. "We haven't been there in ages. I'm surprised you remembered the place."

"Auntie Camille took me there and I like it. The ice cream is super!"

Earlier this spring, Camille, the youngest Hollister sibling, had come up from Red Bluff to stay for a few weeks while her husband, Matthew Waggoner, helped the new foreman settle into his new job. During that visit, Camille had spent extra time with Raine, often taking him with her when she'd made trips into Wickenburg.

"You never told me you liked the Broken Spur that much," Jazelle said thoughtfully.

"It's fun! If you sit at the bar, you can spin the seat around."

"And I'm sure Auntie Camille let you spin your seat around," she said, picturing her son on one of the old red stools.

"Only two times. She said it might break if I did it any more than that."

Thank goodness, Jazelle thought. "Well, if you're a good boy this week, we might go there next Sunday. Today we're going..."

She paused as she realized she didn't know exactly where Connor had planned to take them. He'd simply promised the outing would be something a little boy would enjoy. The idea made her want to roll her eyes. How could a man like him remember being a child? He'd probably come out of the womb winking at the nurses.

"Where, Mommy? To the park? I could swing. That's not as fun as riding Victor, though."

"Today is a surprise. So don't keep asking. Go change out of your church clothes and into the jeans and shirt I put on your bed. And wear your cowboy boots, just in case."

He took off in a run toward his bedroom, yelling questions the whole way. "Just in case of what, Mommy? Are we going to the Bar X?"

With a wry shake of her head, Jazelle called after him, "No more questions."

Three minutes later, her son skidded to a halt just inside the open doorway of her bedroom. "I'm ready," he announced. "See?"

"Almost ready," Jazelle corrected as she walked over to him and stuffed the tails of his cotton shirt into the waistband of his jeans.

Impatient, he wrinkled his nose and squirmed. "Why do I have to have my shirt all fixed? We already went to church this morning. Are we going back again?"

"No. We're going to have company and I want you to look nice. That means you need to brush your hair—yes, again."

He moaned. "Oh, gosh, Mommy, is Grandma coming?"

He didn't sound a bit too happy about that idea, which came as no surprise to Jazelle. Della had never been the gentle, maternal type. Not to her daughter or her grandson. She was constantly scolding Raine and pointing out his faults.

"No. She's not coming. You remember the man you talked to at the ranch? The one who works with Uncle Joe?"

Raine's eyes widened. "Yeah! He's a deputy and his name is Connor."

Finished with his shirt, Jazelle looked at him. "How do you know all that?"

"He told me so."

The night of the dinner party at the ranch, Connor had surprised Jazelle on several counts. First, by carrying the tray upstairs for her and, second, when he'd followed Tessa into the upstairs sitting room. And then while she'd been playing with the twins, she'd noticed Raine approaching Connor. She'd expected the man to briefly acknowledge her son and move on. Instead, he'd squatted to Raine's level and taken the time to have a little conversation with him.

"Oh. I see," Jazelle replied.

Raine went on. "He was resting that night. That's why he wasn't wearing his badge."

"That makes sense," Jazelle said, finger-brushing his thick bangs to one side of his forehead. "Well, Connor is going to be here in a few minutes and take us somewhere nice."

Raine's eyes grew wide and wondrous. "And we'll get to eat with him?"

"Yes, we'll eat with him," Jazelle answered. "Does that sound okay to you?"

A wide smile spread across his face. "Yippee!"

Before Jazelle could say more, he turned and raced out of the room.

"Where are you going?" she called after him.

"I'm going to go watch for Connor!" he yelled back.

Bemused by his reaction, Jazelle turned to the clothes she'd tossed across the foot of the bed. She'd half expected Raine to be resentful or suspicious of having a man show up today. Sunday afternoons were always reserved for just the two of them to spend together. Apparently, the idea of sharing his mother with company didn't bother him.

Thank goodness she wasn't going to have to worry about her son being sulky or petulant, Jazelle thought. Now all she had to do was get through the afternoon without letting Connor Murphy's charm get under her skin.

Last Monday, Connor's work schedule had unexpectedly changed and he'd been forced to put off his date with Jazelle until today. At the time, he'd been terribly disappointed. Especially since he'd had to practically beg her to agree to the outing. But now, after nearly a week had passed, doubts about the whole thing were beginning to creep over him.

He'd be lucky if it didn't turn out to be the most disastrous date he'd ever been on, Connor thought as he drove down the narrow country road to Jazelle's house. Just how many complete sentences could a child of Raine's age put together? And if he behaved in an unruly way, would Jazelle even bother to discipline him? And how was Connor supposed to have any meaningful time with Jazelle if Raine was constantly wedged between them?

This is what happens when you break the rules, Connor. You knew better than to ask Jazelle on a date. You knew she had a child. Yet you barreled on with this plan of yours anyway. You deserve to go home this evening with jangled nerves and a splitting headache.

No way. He wasn't about to let himself reach the point of physical misery. This date with Jazelle was not only going to be the shortest one in his history, Connor promised himself, it was also going to be the final one.

Minutes later, he was parking his truck behind Jazelle's, when he saw Raine racing off the porch and out to greet him.

Grinning, he said in a breathless rush, "Hi, Connor! Mommy said you were coming. I'm glad. Real glad!"

Just when Connor had planned to keep himself emotionally distanced from the little munchkin, the kid had to greet him like this.

Smiling, he said, "I'm glad I'm here, too, Raine. Are you hungry?"

Nodding eagerly, he asked, "Are we gonna eat at the Broken Spur? I like it there, 'cause they have ice cream with brown speckles in it. It's yummy."

Connor tried not to laugh. "The Broken Spur didn't exactly cross my mind. I thought you might like a picnic."

Raine's mouth formed a perfect *O*. "You mean we're gonna sit on a blanket on the floor and eat? Like me and Little Joe do at the ranch? That's what Mommy calls a picnic."

Connor shook his head. "That's what I call a play picnic. I thought we'd go on a real one. That's when you eat outside. How does that sound?"

"Wow! That'll be super-duper!" He grabbed hold

of Connor's hand and tugged him forward. "Come on! Let's go tell Mommy."

Once they were standing in the middle of the small living room, Raine yelled for his mother.

"He's here, Mommy! Come on!"

Connor heard footsteps and looked around as she passed through the open doorway and into the room. Dressed in skinny white jeans that outlined the curvy shape of her legs and hips, and a black peasant blouse that exposed her bare shoulders, she was more than pretty. She was downright sexy.

And he'd planned to make this outing short? He must've been out of his mind.

"Hello, Jazelle. I apologize for being a bit early. The drive over here was shorter than I thought." He sounded like a dumb oaf, but he couldn't help it. With Raine holding on to his hand and Jazelle smiling at him, he felt like he'd turned into a man he'd never met before.

"No problem. I'm almost ready." She gestured to the couch. "Have a seat. If you'd like, Raine will get you something to drink. He's actually as good a waiter as I am a waitress—most of the time."

"Thanks. I'm fine. Just take your time," he told her.

She left the room and Connor eased down onto a dark green couch. Instead of sitting next to him, Raine stood against Connor's leg and rested a little hand on his knee.

"We have lemonade and grape juice," the boy told

him. "Tomato juice, too. But it's yucky. Mommy likes it, though. She likes things that are nu-truscous or something like that."

"You mean 'nutritious'?"

"Yeah. Stuff that's good for you. I like strawberry soda, but she says it makes me hop around like a rabbit."

Connor wondered if it would be okay to laugh or if it would hurt this child's feelings. Either way, he was finding it hard to keep a straight face.

"That's okay," Connor told him. "I'm not thirsty."

Raine tilted his head to one side as he gave Connor a thoughtful look. "Are you resting today?"

"Resting?" he asked. Then, seeing the boy eye his shirt pocket, it dawned on him. "Oh, you mean I'm not wearing my badge today. Well, yes, today is another rest day. So I don't need my badge."

"I like badges," he said. "Someday when I get big, I'm gonna wear one, too. Mommy says you have to be brave and strong to be a lawman. But I can be like that, can't I?"

He had no idea what Jazelle thought about her son growing up to be a lawman. In any case, Raine needed to know he could be just as brave and strong as the next man.

"Sure you can."

Raine scrubbed his nose with the palm of his hand. "I wanta be big like you and Uncle Joe. Then I can take care of Mommy."

That was the last thing Connor had expected to

hear the boy say. How could a little tyke be thinking of such a grown-up thing? He should be running and playing without a serious thought in his head. Was it because he'd never had a father and believed his mother needed a grown-up man to take care of her?

Connor was wondering how to respond when, much to his relief, Jazelle returned to the living room. As soon as she spotted Raine snuggled close to Connor's leg, she paused and stared. Clearly, she hadn't been expecting Raine to make friends with him so quickly. Connor supposed he should've been surprised how the child taken to him, but he wasn't. Never having a mother, and a father who'd only been in his life for a few years, Connor figured there was a connection between him and Raine that only the two of them could understand.

"I'm all set to go," she announced. "Are you two ready?"

Raine trotted over to his mother. "We're going on a picnic. A real one!"

Jazelle's gaze lifted from her son's excited face to Connor's. "A picnic? That's your plan?"

He rose. "Little boys like to be outdoors. So do big ones. But only if the lady of the house agrees," he added.

Her short laugh was a mixture of disbelief and excitement. "I do approve. I, uh, like picnics," she said.

And Connor liked everything he was seeing, he decided. A hint of pink tinged her cheeks and lips, while the hair brushed smooth upon her shoulders was variated shades of gold and sun-kissed wheat. The vibrant color made her brown eyes seem that much darker and richer.

If Raine hadn't been standing at his side, he figured he could've gone on staring at her for long, long minutes. Instead, he cleared his throat and tried to shake himself out of the fog that had suddenly settled in his brain.

"Great. Let's get going," he finally managed to say. "It takes a while to drive to the lake."

Her mouth fell open a second time. "Do you mean Lake Pleasant? We're going that far?"

"That's the nearest lake," he patiently explained. "We don't have time to drive all the way over to Roosevelt."

A frown pulled her brows together. "That's not what I meant. Going that far—it's too much trouble. We could go to the park in town instead," she suggested. "There're picnic tables there and it would save you lots of driving."

She was either a very practical woman or she was thinking to keep their date as short as possible. The thought made him hate himself for planning the same thing.

"That's not my idea of a real picnic. Besides, I thought Raine might like to do a little fishing with me." He looked down at the boy who'd been silently taking in their conversation. "Do you like to fish, Raine?"

Uncertain about answering, the child looked to his mother for help.

"He doesn't know whether he likes it or not," Jazelle explained. "He's never gone fishing."

All sorts of thoughts rushed through Connor's head. The main one being that Raine needed him. The idea was ridiculous, he thought. He was a far cry from father material. But for the boy's sake, he could pretend for a few hours.

Connor reached out and rubbed the top of Raine's head. "No problem. I'm just the guy who can teach him."

While Jazelle cast Connor a doubtful look, Raine hopped around on his toes.

"Yay! I'm going to catch a fish!" he exclaimed.

"We're going to try," Connor corrected him. "Catching a fish isn't always guaranteed."

Jazelle walked over to a wall table and picked up her handbag. "Okay, guys. Looks like we're going to the lake."

Seeing that his mother had given the plan a green light, Raine raced out the front door and left the two adults to follow.

Out on the tiny porch, Connor stood to one side while Jazelle locked the door.

"I hope you're not annoyed with me," he told her.

She glanced at him. "Why would you think I'm annoyed?"

He shrugged one shoulder while wondering why this woman made him feel so uncertain of everything he was doing or saying. She was no different than those he'd dated in the past.

Yeah, who are you trying to kid, Connor? Jazelle is in a whole different league than those women. Furthermore, you know it. So keep your hands to yourself and your mind out of the gutter.

Fighting against the annoying voice in his ear, he said, "Oh, I don't know. Maybe because I didn't make plans to take you and Raine to a nice, family-oriented restaurant. The idea of dealing with ants and dirt and paper plates and—"

"Fresh air and beautiful sunshine sparkling on the lake," she interrupted with a soft smile. "I think I can deal with it okay, Connor."

Relief rushed through him. "I'm glad," he said, thinking he'd never been so manipulated by a woman's brown eyes or soft smile. He was turning into a complete wuss, he decided, then wondered how long it would take Joseph to notice the change in his partner.

Jazelle wasn't very talkative as Connor drove them south from Wickenburg then east onto 74 toward Lake Pleasant State Park. She was using the time to try to figure out the man sitting next to her. As if that were possible, she thought wryly.

Why was he making all this effort to take them to the lake for a picnic? Because he knew Tessa and Joseph would hear about their date and he wanted to impress them. Or did he actually want Raine to feel included and enjoy himself? Since he carried the reputation of being a ladies' man, she found it difficult to believe that the feelings of a five-year-old boy could matter much to him.

"Mommy, are you going to try to catch a fish?" Raine asked from the backseat where Connor had buckled him safely in his booster seat.

"I might leave that up to you, Raine," Jazelle told him. "I haven't tried to fish in a long time. Not since your grandpa Sherman took me fishing years ago. I'd probably get the line all tangled up."

Connor glanced over at her. "We can always get the line untangled," he said then asked, "Did you and your father do much together when you were growing up?"

She nodded. "I was a big daddy's girl and that never changed until Dad…uh, moved away to Oracle. He's lived down there with his other family for a long time now. Ever since he and Mom divorced."

"When did that happen?" he asked.

"When I was thirteen—in junior high school. I have two half-siblings. A ten-year-old brother and eight-year-old sister. I rarely see them or my stepmother, though."

"Why is that? You don't get along with them?"

She shrugged, thinking her family situation was something she rarely discussed with anyone. "We get along well enough. But I wouldn't call us close. They've only been to Wickenburg a handful of times.

And I've been down there to see them even less. I guess it's just too awkward for everyone involved."

She turned her gaze at the landscape whizzing by the passenger window. It had been ages since she'd gone past the town of Wickenburg or beyond Three Rivers Ranch. Seeing the beautiful desert with its thick green chaparral, tall saguaros and distant mountains was always a treat. But today the majestic landscape wasn't enough to blot out the sexy image of the man sitting next to her.

"I don't know how you feel," Connor said, "but I resented my dad for leaving me behind. Even though he didn't have a choice in the matter. He died."

His blunt remark had her turning her head to stare at him. "Your father died?"

"I had just entered high school when he had a heart attack. He was never sick, so that made it even more of a shock. After that, I got bounced around to different relatives until I became legal age. Then I moved out on my own."

The sound of his voice held no emotion. Was that because he was a lawman who'd been trained to keep his emotions in check and all statements stripped down to just the facts? Or was he hiding his real feelings behind a protective wall, the way she often tried to do?

"You said you were bounced around. What about your mother?" she asked, more curious about this man's life than she had a right to be.

"Never knew the woman. She was a juvenile delinquent and, after she gave birth to me, she walked away and never came back."

Jazelle was stunned. What little she knew about Connor had come from Tessa and she'd never mentioned anything about his family or lack of one. Jazelle had just assumed he'd come from a typical, happy family.

"Oh. I'm sorry," she said awkwardly. "I shouldn't have asked."

"Why should you be sorry? It's hardly a secret." He cast her a rueful smile. "You're probably thinking I should sound a little more cut up about the situation. But you can't grieve for something you never had, Jazelle."

"No. I guess it would be hard to miss a mother you never knew," she said then shrugged. "My dad—he did leave by his own choice. And maybe I do resent him a little for that. But he tried his best to get custody of me. Mom fought him all the way. Until he just finally gave up."

"Gave up? I don't think I could ever do that. Not with my own child," he said.

How would this man know what he would do in those same circumstances? she wondered. He'd never been married, much less had a child of his own. When it came to families coming together or falling apart, nothing about it was simple. Just like his mother walking away. He'd made her leaving sound simple. Yet, underneath, Jazelle figured there had to be layers of pain and resentment involved with her abandonment.

Deciding now would be the perfect time for Raine to interrupt with a slew of questions, Jazelle glanced over her shoulder to see her son was gazing out the window. He was so transfixed by sights he'd never seen before, he wasn't paying any attention to the adults in the front seat.

Turning her gaze back to Connor, she said, "You're probably thinking my father must've been a wimp to have caved in to my mother. He wasn't. He was—is—a laid-back guy. But Mom is the op-posite and when she gets hold of something she's like a bulldog. She won't let go, even if she should. She's the kind who has to win and has to be right. My father was tired of living under that kind of stress. He wanted to be happy. If that meant giving up on me… Well, I can't resent him for that. But I do still miss him. A lot."

He slanted her another glance. "You're a much better person than I am, Jazelle. I still can't forgive my dad for dying and leaving me."

What about his mother? Jazelle wondered. She was the one who deserved Connor's bitterness. But perhaps he was right; he couldn't feel anything for a person he'd never known.

After a moment she said, "I'm a bit surprised about you and me."

Connor didn't glance in her direction, but the

truck suddenly slacked in speed and Jazelle figured her remark must have caught him off guard.

"What's surprising about the two of us?

"That we're alike—as far as our parents are concerned," she explained. "We both lost out in that department."

He let out a long breath, as though he'd been expecting her to say something he wasn't ready to hear. Like what? she wondered. What could she possibly say to him that a woman hadn't already said?

Smiling, he looked over at her. "I think you and I have turned out okay, don't you?"

What was it about this man that made her feel so warm and special? Why did she feel the urge to reach over and touch him? To connect herself to him even in the smallest of ways? The feelings were more than odd to her. They were downright scary.

Smiling wanly, she said, "Put that way, I guess we have."

Before they reached the lake, Connor expected Raine to start complaining of the long drive and whining to get out of the truck. Instead, he'd remained fairly quiet, only remarking when he spotted a few wild donkeys grazing on a hillside and another time when they passed a restaurant parking lot filled with motorcycles.

"Is he normally this quiet when you're traveling?" Connor asked in a low, puzzled voice.

From the corner of his eye, Connor could see Jazelle shake her head. "Not hardly. It's usually non-stop chatter. But we never go any farther than Three Rivers. Right now he's entranced by all the new sights."

"I'm glad. I was afraid he was getting bored and sulking."

"He's not that type. Being an only child, he's learned how to entertain himself. He's also learned that sulking will get him nowhere," she said then emitted a soft laugh. "Sorry. I probably sound like a bragging parent. Truthfully, it's not easy and I'm not perfect."

Connor chuckled. "I've never been good at being perfect. Just ask Joe."

Raine suddenly called out, "Mommy, look at all the water! And boats. Lots of them!"

"That's the lake," Jazelle told her son. Gesturing her head toward the back seat, she said to Connor, "See. He's coming alive now."

"We're about to cross the dam," he told the boy. "It won't be long now until we're there."

While Raine clapped his hands with excitement, Jazelle asked, "Where is 'there'?"

"Oh, to a quiet little spot where Joe and I used to go fishing back before work and his family obligations took up our recreation time. It's not a regular camping area with a picnic table," he explained. "We'll have to eat off the ground. But it is nice, private, and partially shaded. Sound okay? Or would you rather go somewhere more public where you can eat at a table?"

She gave him an impish smile. "Connor, I have to set tables every day at the ranch. It'll be nice not to have to deal with one today. And Raine's never had a real picnic on the ground before. This will be a first for him."

This day was turning out to have plenty of firsts for Connor, too, he thought. For the first time in his life he was taking a single mother and her child on a family excursion. And, wonder of wonders, he was enjoying every moment of it.

"Then I hope he isn't disappointed," he told her. "Once we're on the other side of the dam, it won't take us too long to get to where we're going."

Fifteen minutes later, after skirting the edge of the lake and several public campgrounds, Connor steered the truck off the asphalt road and onto a narrow dirt track that led through a series of low hills covered with sage, tall cacti and thorny chaparral.

Eventually they reached a private cove sheltered on two sides with tall rocky bluffs. Water gently lapped at a small stretch of beach shaded with a few shrubby mesquite trees.

"Okay, Raine. We're here," Connor told the boy as he parked the truck in an out-of-the-way place and shut off the motor. "Ready to get out?"

Bubbling with eagerness, Raine practically shouted, "Oh, boy, yeah! I can't wait!"

Connor glanced at Jazelle. "Don't move," he told

her. "I'll help Raine out first. Otherwise, he's going to burst."

While Connor unbuckled the boy's seat belt, Jazelle went over the dos and don'ts she expected her son to follow.

"And if you go near the water without me or Connor with you, then you're going to be in very serious trouble," Jazelle added firmly. "Plus, I'll have Connor pack everything up and take us home."

"Wow, Raine, your mother sounds very serious." Connor plucked Raine from the seat and set him on the ground. "I think you'd better do what she says, don't you? Or we might end up going home before we ever get to catch a fish."

Raine grinned impishly up at Connor. "I'll be good. I promise!"

The child skipped off to explore a ring of stones someone had put together for a fire and Connor moved up to the passenger door, where Jazelle was waiting for him to help her down from the truck.

When she placed her hand in his and gracefully stepped onto the ground beside him, Connor was highly tempted to slip his arm around the back of her waist and pull her close to his side. But, hell, he'd barely managed to talk her into this innocent outing. She wouldn't appreciate him trying to put a move on her.

Even so, he decided to push his luck and keep her hand enfolded in his for a few more moments. "I hope this meets your approval," he said.

Her gaze lifted to his and Connor was surprised to see a wicked little glint in the brown depths. "Are you talking about the way you're holding my hand," she asked, "or this picnic spot?"

Hoping his smile didn't look as sheepish as it felt, he said, "I was asking about the cove. But I'd be mighty interested to hear your opinion on the hand-holding, too."

"The cove is absolutely beautiful. Thank you for bringing us here," she said. Then her fingers tightened ever so slightly around his. "As for the hand-holding, it's been a long, long time since I've touched a man like this. It's nice. But very scary."

From the very first moment Connor had laid eyes on Jazelle, he'd recognized she was different. Yet it wasn't until this very moment that he realized just how different she was from the other women he'd dated. And suddenly all that mattered to him was making her feel safe and protected. And happy.

"You shouldn't be scared, Jazelle," he said gently. "Not of me."

Her thumb softly moved against the back of his hand. "It's not just you that worries me, Connor. I don't exactly trust myself—with you."

Connor realized there were several layers to the meaning of her words and though he desperately wanted to know what she was thinking and feeling, he wasn't going to push her. For now, he simply wanted to enjoy being close to her and to let himself imagine how it might be if he ever decided to become a one-woman man.

Chapter Six

"Can I have another piece of chicken, Mommy?"

Jazelle looked over to the corner of the plaid blanket where Raine was sitting cross-legged. Except for a few bones and a spoonful of macaroni and cheese, the paper plate balanced on his lap was empty.

"I've never seen you eat this much, Raine," she told him. "Are you sure you can hold another piece of chicken?"

"Sure he can." Connor spoke up. "He's a growing boy and being outdoors makes a person hungrier."

"Yeah, Mommy! I'm growing! Connor said I'll get big like him."

Her son was usually a happy child, but today joy was shining on his face and the sight filled her heart.

"Okay, big boy. One more piece." Jazelle fished a leg from a sack containing the fried chicken and handed it to Raine. "But eat it, don't waste it."

After returning the sack to a large picnic basket, she shut the lid and looked over at Connor.

"Obviously this basket isn't new, so I know you didn't just go out and buy it. Exactly what is a man like you doing with a traditional picnic basket?"

He chuckled. "You mean I don't look the type?"

She cast him a shrewd smile. "Uh…not exactly."

Shrugging, he said, "Actually, I haven't used the thing in years. Not since Joe and I used to fish. We used it to carry our food and fishing lures."

She ran an appreciative hand over the smooth woven wicker. "Oh, then you've had it a long time," she remarked.

He nodded. "It belonged to my grandmother Lottie. She used it to store her knitting stuff."

Jazelle recalled him saying he'd been bounced back and forth between relatives, but she didn't recall him mentioning a grandmother. "Is your grandmother still living?" she asked curiously.

"No. Not long after my father passed away, she died. The basket was one of her belongings that I wanted to keep." He let out a long sigh. "She was a sweet woman who never had much of a life. Her husband—Granddad—was a rigid man. He'd always wanted to be in the military, but was rejected for a hearing problem. After that, he never cared much about anything. Lottie mostly paid the bills by working as a cafeteria cook at the high school. Granddad lives over in Maricopa County now."

"What about your mother's parents? Do they live around here?" she asked.

He grimaced. "From what Dad told me, my mother ran away from home, which she'd told him was somewhere in Nevada. He never learned who her parents were or where they actually lived. You see, she and my dad were only hooked up for a brief time. I guess long enough for him to figure out she was nothing but trouble."

She studied Connor's solemn face, while thinking it was a miracle that, after such a rough start in life, he'd grown up to be a respectable lawman. "Oh. Then they weren't together when you were born?"

"No. He didn't even know she was expecting. It wasn't until she'd abandoned me that Dad learned of my existence. That's when he stepped in and took me home." He looked at her. "What about your grandparents? Are they living?"

She sipped from a can of soda before she answered. "They all live far away. My mom's folks are in a little town in north Michigan and dad's parents live up near Seattle. I haven't seen any of them in several years. My mother never was very close to her parents. Dad's parents travel down to Arizona fairly often, but they go to Oracle. They don't, uh, bother to come by and see me or their great-grandson."

"Why not?"

Jazelle shrugged. "I don't know exactly. I expect

it's because they despise how Mom treated their son while she and Dad were married. And how she fought him tooth-and-nail over custody of me."

"You or Raine hardly had anything to do with that," he pointed out.

"No. But we represent all those bad times. And it's much easier for them to just focus on Dad's other... good family."

"Does that bother you?"

"It used to—when I was much younger," she admitted. "But not anymore. I have the Hollisters. They're my family now."

He placed his empty plate aside and, stretching back on one elbow, looked over at Raine who was chomping at the last of the chicken leg.

"The Hollisters are a pretty great bunch," he said. "Joe is like my brother. Even when we were kids, he always had my back and I had his. It's still that way."

Beneath lowered lashes, Jazelle allowed her gaze to travel up and down his tall, muscular frame. A pair of faded, worn jeans molded to his thighs, while a moss-green button-up shirt stretched across a pair of broad shoulders. The sleeves were rolled back slightly on his forearms, allowing her a peek at the hard-corded muscle and the dark blond hair sprinkled over the tops. Every inch of him oozed masculinity and Jazelle caught herself wondering what he would look like without the casual clothing.

Clearing her throat, she said, "Well, I expect that Joe has a certain connection with you that he'll never have with his brothers. Because you two are lawmen together."

"Maybe. But his brothers mean the world to him, too. So does his mom."

Jazelle considered asking him about the investigation into Joel's death, but she didn't want to darken the afternoon with such talk. And, anyway, Raine suddenly jumped to his feet.

"Can we go fishing now, Connor?" he asked.

"Connor might not be finished eating, Raine," Jazelle told him. "He hasn't had dessert yet. Neither have you. And I saw cookies and cake in the picnic basket."

"I'm too full." Raine pointed to an outcropping of rocks a few yards away from the picnic blanket. "While I wait on Connor, can I walk over there?"

"You may," she told him. "But don't go any further than that tree behind the rocks."

"Okay!"

The boy took off in a run to the rocks and Connor chuckled as he watched him go. "I think he's having fun."

"This is far better than a toy store to him." Jazelle gave him a meaningful smile. "I'm very grateful to you, Connor, for going to all this trouble. He'll talk about this day for a long time to come."

"There's no need for you to keep thanking me, Jazelle. This outing isn't just for Raine. It's for you and me, too." He straightened to a sitting position and, after digging a bag of cookies from the basket, he offered it to Jazelle. "Want one?

She shook her head. "No, thanks. I'm stuffed. I've probably made more of a pig of myself than Raine. And now that we're on the subject of eating, you should've told me you were planning a picnic so I could help with the food."

He grinned. "Forget it. I didn't mind slaving over the stove all morning. It was nothing really."

Knowing he was teasing, she playfully arched her brows at him. "A real picnic basket and all this cooking, too? I'm shocked."

He chuckled. "Okay. I confess. I worked really hard choosing what to get at the deli. Actually, if boiling water didn't bubble, I wouldn't know when to turn off the burner."

No, he hardly looked like he belonged in the kitchen, Jazelle thought. But she could certainly conjure up images of him in the bedroom, stretched out on a sheet, wearing nothing but a glint in his eyes. It wasn't hard to figure out how he'd managed to go through women like a bowlful of bite-size candies. And it would be very easy to let herself become one more bite. But she couldn't give in to those kinds of urges. Not with a man like Connor, who'd only stick around for a few days and then be gone. Still, it was nice to dream, if only for a day.

She was trying to push the dangerous thoughts aside when Raine suddenly called out, "Mommy! Come look! I found a worm!"

Thankful for the interruption, Jazelle quickly rose from the blanket and brushed the crumbs off the front of her jeans. "Raine loves worms, but I'd better go make sure his worm isn't actually a snake. That's happened more than once."

As Connor watched her walk over the uneven ground, he decided he must be a first-class fool. A bum didn't have a chance of making a princess fall in love with him, so what in heck had made him think he could get past first base with Jazelle?

Whoa, Connor. Who said anything about falling in love? When did that thought even come into the picture? You need to get your head twisted on straight. Otherwise, you're setting yourself up for a huge crash.

Disgusted with the crazy and negative thoughts circling in his head, Connor left the blanket and walked over to where Raine was using a small stick to poke at something on the ground.

"Where is this critter you found?" he asked the boy.

"It fell off the tree and landed right in there." He pointed to a crevice between two roots. "It's white and fuzzy. Can I put it in a jar and keep it?

"We don't have a jar, sweetie," Jazelle pointed out.

Connor peered down at the thing that had caught Raine's attention and immediately took the boy by the shoulders and pulled him aside. "I hate to spoil your fun, Raine, but that bug isn't anything to play with. It's poisonous and if it touches you, it hurts really awful. So don't ever try to catch one."

Jazelle cast Connor a fearful glance. "What is it?"

"They're called asps. It's a type of caterpillar that's covered with tiny feathers—at least, they look like feathers," he explained. "When they stick in a person's skin, it stings something fierce. Sometimes the stings can be very dangerous."

Jazelle groaned. "Oh, Lord, it's not enough to have to worry about Raine finding a sidewinder or Gila monster. Now I have to worry about asps," she said. On a more hopeful note, she asked, "Do they only live by the water?"

"No. They usually stay in trees and shrubs—anywhere outdoors. I'm just glad Raine was smart enough not to pick this one up without asking first." Connor patted the top of the Raine's head. "Good boy."

Raine looked up at him as though he was a caped crusader who'd just saved him from an evil villain. "From now on, if I find a snake or bug or lizard, I'm gonna run fast!"

Jazelle sighed with relief as she looked over at Connor.

"Thank you," she said. "Especially for explaining the dangers to Raine. Coming from you, they'll more likely stick in his head."

Connor suddenly felt a foot taller and wondered if that was the way a man felt when he had a woman who adored him, who believed in him, and wanted him at her side. Did a man ever get tired of wanting to be a hero to the woman he loved? He'd never know, Connor thought wryly.

"I don't want the little man to get hurt. Not if I can help it."

The smile Jazelle gave him was so sweet it caused an ache to rifle right through his chest.

In an effort to ease it, Connor coughed and settled a hand on Raine's shoulder. "How about trying our hand at fishing now?" he asked. "The sun is high, but the fish might bite anyway."

Raine looked eagerly up at him. "Does a fish know about the sun? How can he? He's under the water."

Connor laughed. "A fish sees lights and shadows. And he likes to swim around in the shadows."

"Then we might find one there. A big one!" Raine exclaimed.

"I hope we do. If you catch a big one, maybe your mom will cook it for our supper," Connor suggested, giving Jazelle a wink to assure her she probably wasn't in any danger of having to cook a fish.

"Yeah. That would be super fun," Raine said. "She can cook fish really good. And she squeezes lemon juice over it. That makes it yummy!"

Jazelle smiled impishly at the both of them. "I'd be glad to cook fish for the two of you. But I think you should catch a string of them first."

Connor played along with her. "That sounds like

a challenge, Raine. We'll just have to show her what good fishermen we are."

"Yeah. And Mommy can take a picture so I can show Little Joe!"

Connor looked over at Jazelle. "Sounds like I have my work cut out for me."

She laughed lightly and Connor decided the sound was like tinkling bells at Christmas, filled with the promise of joy to come. Just hearing it could be addictive, he thought.

"Sounds like I might have a bit of work ahead of me, too," she said.

At that moment, Raine grabbed Connor's hand and tugged him forward. "Come on, Connor! Let's run!"

Chuckling, Connor almost felt like a kid again as he trotted with Raine to the truck, where the fishing gear was lying on the tailgate ready and waiting.

Nearly two hours later, Raine had worn himself down and was asleep on the picnic blanket. A few feet away, Jazelle and Connor sat on a bleached-out log. In front of them, the water gently lapped upon the rocky shoreline, while in the distance boats bobbled on the waves.

Now that the sun had lowered, the fierce heat had eased and the wind off the water felt cool against Jazelle's skin. But it wasn't enough to temper the heat radiating from the man sitting at her side. Each time his shoulder casually came in contact with hers, she felt as though a flame was licking her face.

Throughout the afternoon, Jazelle had been assuring herself that this afternoon with Connor was only a casual outing. Nothing more, or less. But so far everything about this day was turning out to be nothing like she'd planned. Slowly but surely she could feel herself drawing closer and closer to the sexy deputy.

"I'm sorry that Raine didn't catch a big fish," he said. "He had his hopes up high. I feel like I let him down."

The sound of his voice interrupted her swirling thoughts and she looked over at him. "Are you kidding? Just catching a small fish put him over the moon. And I appreciate you teaching him that the little fish have to be turned back into the water. Whether he ever goes fishing again or not, he needs to know the rules and understand that he has to follow them. Or a man with a badge might give him a ticket," she added teasingly.

"Aw. And he believes men with badges are all nice guys." He grinned and then said in a more serious tone, "Might surprise you to know that I'd once planned to become a game ranger."

"I can't picture you in that mild-mannered role."

Her remark caused him to chuckle. "Parks and wildlife rangers are hardly mild-mannered. When it comes to criminals and breaking the law, a game ranger has just as much authority as any other lawman. And they probably get involved in more dangerous situations than the normal deputy sheriff. Poachers with rifles and fugitives trying to hide in the wilderness make for some wild encounters."

Jazelle hated to admit it, but she was totally intrigued by the man. She wanted to know what he was thinking, not just about her and Raine, but about a jillion other things about him and his life.

She said, "Obviously you changed your mind and joined the Yavapai sheriff's department. How did that happen?"

He shrugged. "Joe. He wanted to be a deputy sheriff and had the cockeyed idea that we might end up as partners. Just the idea of getting to work with my best friend was enough for me to shelve my plan to be a game warden."

"Do you regret the choice?" she asked.

He shook his head. "No. Even though we both had several different partners before we finally got the chance to pair up."

She gave him an understanding nod. "It makes everything better when you're partnered with the right person. Reeva and I are a team. I can't imagine working without her."

He said, "I didn't see Reeva the other night when I was at the ranch for dinner. Joe often mentions her and raves about her cooking. I've met her before— a long time ago, but never really visited with her."

"She's seventy-three now. But she's more like fifty-three."

He slanted her a wry look. "In other words, she doesn't act old and crotchety?"

Jazelle chuckled. "Oh, she can get crotchety when she gets upset about something. But that's not too often. And we understand where one another is coming from. You know what I mean?"

To her surprise, he reached over and gathered her hand between his. The warm, rough skin of his palm pressed to hers sent all sorts of delicious thoughts through her head and suddenly her heart was pounding with anticipation. For what, she didn't know exactly. With Raine lying only a few feet away, it wasn't like they were alone, or that he was even thinking about kissing her. But she was thinking about it. Far too much.

"I do know," he murmured. "But I can't begin to guess where you're coming from—what you're thinking about me or about being here with me."

Jazelle's heart began to beat even faster and she wondered if he had any idea of how he was affecting her. He couldn't possibly guess that he was the first and only man since Spence who'd caused any sort of reaction in her.

"Would you like me to be totally honest? Or just nice?" she asked.

His low chuckle was completely sexy and it slipped down her spine like a pair of fingertips walking over her skin.

"I think I'd prefer the honest answer," he said.

"Even though I'm guessing the nice one might be better for my ego."

His hold on her hand hadn't loosened. If anything, his fingers had tightened around hers and yet she didn't feel the need to pull away from him. Rather, she wanted to keep touching him. She wanted to continue gazing into his sky-blue eyes and listening to the deep timbre of his voice.

Something in her throat was fluttering, forcing her to swallow before she could manage to utter a word. "Okay, the honest answer is that I didn't expect to like you. But I do. And when you took hold of my hand a minute ago, I wasn't planning on feeling the things I'm feeling right now."

One of his brows arched faintly while a dimple appeared near the corner of his lips. He was so damned handsome, she thought. Just looking at him was enough to get a woman so rattled she wouldn't know what she was doing or saying. And Jazelle feared she'd almost reached that point.

"What are you feeling right now?"

The low, gravelly tone of his voice made her want to close her eyes and lean into him. It made her want to forget all about the heartache and pain she'd endured because of a man's touch.

"Surprise, mostly," she admitted to him. "Since Raine's father walked out of my life, I haven't wanted any man to touch me. Not for any reason. But I— it feels different with you somehow."

She watched his features soften as his gaze traveled intimately over her face and it almost felt like he was kissing her with eyes. The notion jangled her senses to the point that she could scarcely remember to breathe.

"Since you're being honest, maybe I should do a little confessing, too," he murmured. "This past week, I've been kicking myself for asking you out. You see, it's my policy not to date women with children. I mean it *was* a rule of mine—until you—until today."

When she didn't make any reply to that, he said, "But I'm very glad I decided to go against my self-imposed rules. Raine has been a joy. I didn't know being with a kid could be fun."

Tilting her head to one side, Jazelle regarded his face, which seemed to be drawing closer to hers with each passing second. "You have something against children?"

"No. It's just that I didn't have my dad for very long in my life. Not long enough to learn how to be a dad, that's for sure. And until Joe had kids of his own, I was never around any." His expression turned a bit guilty. "I'm supposed to be being honest, aren't I?"

Nodding, she said, "I'd appreciate it if you were."

"Okay. There's more to it than just not knowing how to interact with kids. I've learned that a single mom is usually looking for a permanent partner— a daddy for her son or daughter. I'm not the right man to fill that bill, so I keep my distance. And now you're thinking I'm a real selfish bastard, aren't you?" he asked ruefully.

She shook her head. "No. I'm thinking you're being honest. I'm thinking you're a man who knows his limitations. And you don't want to hurt yourself or anyone else by trying to step out of the parameters you've set up for yourself."

A look of genuine surprise swept over his features. "You really do get it, don't you?"

"I do. Except for one thing," she told him. "Why did you decide to break your rule with me?"

His fingers lifted just enough to draw gentle circles against the back of her hand. The sensation caused goose bumps to erupt along her arms.

"Because I really like you. And I could see that you're different. You're not interested in a serious relationship or on a hunt for a husband. I figured you and I could enjoy each other's company without a bunch of expectations. The kind that always fall flat."

Why did she feel so deflated? She'd known from the very beginning that his intentions weren't serious. Nor would they ever be. "You mean if we don't expect anything, we won't be disappointed?"

He looked almost thrilled. "Wow! You're reading my mind."

She refrained from rolling her eyes. "I read your mind the first time I ever met you."

His happy grin turned into a confused scowl. "What does that mean?"

"It just means that as soon as we met, I recognized what you wanted from a woman."

"Oh," he said. "What's that?"

"A good time. Nothing more. Nothing less."

A ruddy color washed onto his face. "If that's what you thought, then why did you agree to go out with me today?"

She gave him a clever smile. "I guess you could say I used you to break the monotony. It's not often that I'm given the chance to get away from home or work. And have a free meal, to boot."

He must have picked up on the teasing twinkle in her eyes because a wry grin slowly lifted one corner of his mouth. "Hmm. If an outing was all you wanted, you could've made a trip to the grocery store."

Jazelle had to laugh. "Sorry, Connor. I was teasing about that last part. About breaking the monotony and the meal."

"I guess I should be thankful for that much," he said dryly.

The playful smile on her face vanished and she gently placed her hand on top of his. "Actually, I came out with you today because I thought I would enjoy your company. Plus, I knew I'd be safe."

"Safe?" he repeated quizzically.

"Well, yes. You don't want anything serious from me. And I don't expect it from you. It's all for fun."

Jazelle had expected her explanation to bring a huge smile to his face. Instead, he merely looked at her as though she'd been trying to talk him through a trigonometry equation.

He dropped his hold on her hand and gazed pensively out at the lake. "Fun. Yeah," he finally said. "You're right. That's all this is. Just fun for me and you and Raine."

The sudden change in him perplexed her, but she wasn't about to press him for an explanation. Frankly, his feelings shouldn't matter to her one way or the other. After today, she doubted he'd ask her out again and, even if he did, she'd have to think long and hard before she'd accept a second date from him. Being with the man was too risky to her common sense.

But that didn't mean she wanted to cut this time with him short. "I'm not sure how early you wanted to get back home, but before the day is over, there's something I'd like to do," she told him. "That is, after Raine wakes and if you're game."

That brought his head back around to hers and he looked at her with interest. "What's that?"

She gestured to the rocky bluff that rose behind them. "I thought it would be fun to hike up to the top of the bluff. I imagine the view is spectacular up there and Raine loves to climb."

The look on his face was an odd mixture of happiness and relief.

"I'm not in any hurry to go home," he assured her. "We'll hike as far as you'd like. In fact, there are some Native American ruins not far behind this bluff. Raine might find a real arrowhead there. Would he like doing something like that?"

In spite of all the warnings about this man that had been swirling around in her head, she couldn't stop herself from squeezing his hand and smiling. "You know what I'm beginning to think about you?" she asked.

"I couldn't begin to guess."

The smile on her face deepened. "You've been fibbing to me."

His brows pulled together. "About what?"

"You said you weren't good at interacting with kids. But I see differently. You instinctively seem to know the things Raine would enjoy."

His expression turned sheepish. "That's only because—like I told you the other night at Three Rivers—I was a little boy once. I've been trying to remember back that far and put myself in Raine's place."

"Well, you're doing a good job of it."

His gaze connected with hers and, for a split second, she forgot to breathe as she spotted something in his eyes that had nothing to do with sexual attraction. No, it was much more than a man wanting a woman. It was like he'd suddenly exposed an inner part of himself to her, and she couldn't look away or think beyond the moment.

"I've been learning something about you, too," he murmured.

"What's that?" she asked, her voice barely above a whisper.

"That you're far too nice to be out with a guy like me. But I'm glad you are."

She finally remembered to breathe and a rush of air swooshed past her lips. "I'm glad I am, too."

Chapter Seven

When Connor parked the truck in front of Jazelle's house much later that evening, it had been dark for more than two hours and Raine was sound asleep in the backseat.

"No need for you to wake him," Connor said as he helped Jazelle to the ground. "You go ahead and unlock the door. I'll carry Raine inside for you."

Nodding, she fished the house key from her handbag and hurried on to the little porch.

Connor opened the back door of the truck where Raine's head had fallen against one side of the booster seat. After gently removing the confining straps, he scooped the child out of the seat then used his shoulder to shove the truck door shut.

Once inside the house, Jazelle motioned for him to follow her. "Come this way and I'll show you where to put him."

Connor followed her out of the living room and down a short passageway. To the right, she entered an open door and switched on a lamp at the head of a single bed.

While she pulled the cover back and straightened the pillow, Connor stood to one side and tried not to think about the warm weight of the boy cradled in his arms, or the way it felt to have his little cheek pressed against his chest. What had his own father been thinking all those years ago when he'd carried Connor in his arms? Love? Protectiveness? Or had he been reminded of the mistake he'd made with the wrong woman?

Drawing in a deep breath, Connor pushed the hurtful thought away and glanced around the small room. For a child of Raine's age, he'd expected to see a few toys and pieces of clothing scattered around on the floor. Instead, it was surprisingly neat, almost to the point of being bare.

"Okay. The bed is ready."

Jazelle's voice broke into his musings and he moved forward to ease the child onto the narrow mattress.

"What about his clothes?" he asked, careful not to allow his voice above a whisper.

"I'll deal with them later," she told him.

As if on cue, Raine suddenly roused from his

slumber and gazed sleepily up at Connor. "I found a real arrowhead."

"That's right, little buddy. Now go back to sleep." Connor gently stroked the child's forehead until his blue eyes drifted closed. When his breathing grew slow and even, he glanced up at Jazelle. "I think he's gone back to sleep."

Nodding, Jazelle started to pull off his boots and it was then that Connor noticed Raine was clutching something in his right hand.

Gently, he opened the little fingers to find the piece of flint hewed to the shape of an arrowhead. Raine had been ecstatic when he'd found the rock and had chattered about it until he'd fallen asleep on the way home. Such simple things today had made the boy so very happy, he thought.

Connor straightened away from the bed and handed Jazelle the arrowhead. "Here," he said. "Raine was still holding on to this. I think you might want to put it up for him."

Smiling wanly, she looked down at the rock resting in the middle of her palm. "I think he was just as thrilled over finding this as he was about catching a fish."

She placed the arrowhead on top of a chest of drawers, then drew the cover over Raine. "I know his clothes are dirty and he needs a bath, but I don't think it will hurt him to sleep like this just one time."

He smiled at her. "Never did hurt me."

"That's good to know." She switched off the lamp

and, after she turned on a nightlight, the two of them slipped out of the room and into the short hallway.

As they migrated toward the living room, Connor told himself it was time he put an end to the evening. He was feeling far too comfortable and contented in her company. It wasn't normal. *He* was no longer normal.

"Well, I need to be leaving," he said, literally forcing the words out of his mouth. "I'm sure you probably have to be at work early in the morning."

"I do. But it's not yet bedtime. Would you like a cup of coffee or something before you go?"

The invitation took him by complete surprise and he paused in the shadowy hallway to glance at her. "Are you sure you're not making the offer just to be polite?"

Stopping alongside him, she shot him an impatient look. "I'm not that prim and polite, Connor. If I wanted you to leave I'd tell you goodbye and shut the door behind you."

"Ouch. That's plain enough," he said then grinned. "Okay, I'd love some coffee before I drive up to Wilhoit."

She said, "Come on with me to the kitchen. We'll sit at the table—if that's okay with you?"

As long as she was in his sight, everything was okay with him, Connor thought, immediately wondering if he'd left part of his mind back at the lake. He felt like a moonstruck idiot wandering around with a goofy grin on his face.

"Sure. I can even make the coffee, if you like."

He followed her over to another open doorway, where a light over the cookstove shed a dim glow across the kitchen cabinets.

As they entered the room, she said in a teasing voice, "I thought you had trouble boiling water. How would you know how to make coffee?"

He chuckled. "Joe forced me to learn. We have a coffeemaker in our office and he thought it was only fair that we shared the chore."

"You two have an office of your own?"

"Well, it's nothing special. In fact, it's a small space. But we managed to fit two desks in it and a few file cabinets."

She switched a light on over the sink and then pulled down a large can of coffee from a shelf near the stove.

She said, "I thought file cabinets were obsolete nowadays."

He crossed the room to stand next to her. "Not all archived cases and information has been stored on computer," he told her. "At least, not yet anyway. Honestly, I prefer digging out a folder with written statements. Especially the information that's been jotted down by hand. There's something about it that makes everything more real and personal."

As she heaped coffee grounds into a filter, she said, "I wasn't going to bring this up, but now that you mentioned Joe and your office, I can't resist. I'm wondering about the investigation into Joel's death.

Reeva believes Joe has asked for your help—that's why you came to dinner the other night."

"He's kept me in the loop of things all along. But he's asked me to help him make an all-out push to find Joel's killer, and I'm only too glad to devote my off hours to the cause. None of the Hollisters will truly rest until the case is solved and closed once and for all."

"You're right about that. From the things Maureen says at times…well, I think the not knowing still keeps her in a bit of a limbo. Otherwise, I think she would've already become engaged to Gil."

Her comment surprised him and he wondered if Jazelle was simply viewing the situation through romantic eyes. "You honestly think so? Joe hasn't mentioned anything about Gil and his mother. Except that she's come to rely on him."

"Maybe Joe doesn't want to see the writing on the wall. But any way you look at it, Maureen is in love with Gil. And vice versa."

"You say that like you know it's a fact."

"Most everyone on Three Rivers knows it," she said and then cast him a rueful glance. "For her sake, I wish you and Joe could uncover the truth. That would make lots of people happy."

"Me included," he admitted. "I can tell you one thing, if someone had murdered my father, I'd damned well want to find him and make sure he never saw the outside of a penitentiary."

She poured water into the coffee machine and

pushed the on button before she turned to face him. "I'm sorry, Connor. I shouldn't have brought up such a gloomy subject. It's not a good way to end our day, which I think turned out to be very nice, don't you?"

Nice? That was putting it mildly, Connor thought. He felt as if he'd just gone through some life-changing event. One that scared the hell out of him.

His heart suddenly beating fast, he took a step toward her. "I've enjoyed it very much. Too much… I think."

She tilted her head back to look up at him. "There can never be too much joy, Connor."

Oh, yes, there could be, he thought. Especially when the abundance of happiness was over something he could never have for himself.

"I, uh, can only think of one other thing that could make it better," he murmured.

Her eyes widened and Connor was thankful that she couldn't read his mind. Otherwise, she'd probably be running from the kitchen.

"I can't imagine what that might be," she said, her gaze never wavering from his.

Connor took one more step forward and then, before she had time to guess his intentions, he bent his head and captured her lips beneath his.

The sudden contact produced a tiny moan somewhere deep in her throat, but that was her only response, until he wrapped his arms around her shoulders and pulled her close against him.

At that point, he expected her to jerk away and

give him a scathing speech about behaving like a cad. He even imagined her palm cracking against his cheek. But none of those things happened. Instead, he was shocked senseless by the hungry movement of her soft mouth beneath his lips, the feel of her slender arms wrapping around his waist.

He was still breathing, so he couldn't be in heaven, he realized, but he had to be darned close to paradise. The taste of her lips and the scent of her skin and hair mingled together to create a euphoric reaction in his brain. And then there was the way the soft curves of her body molded against his, the way the heat of her skin spread through his hands and shot up his arms.

Connor was so lost in her kiss, he was clueless about the time ticking by or the pungent scent of coffee filling the kitchen. The only thought in his brain was to deepen the kiss, to hold her so close that the two of them became inseparable.

Somewhere in the back of his muddled mind, he recognized the circle of her arms tightening around his waist, the groan in her throat growing deeper and louder. This was exactly what he wanted from her, he thought. It was *all* he wanted from her.

You're lying, Connor. You want more than sex from this woman. Why can't you admit, at least to yourself, that she means more to you than a romp in bed?

The voice rattling around in his head was enough to snap him into reality and he quickly broke the contact of their lips and stepped back from her.

"I—I'm sorry, Jazelle. I need to go. You'll have to drink the coffee without me."

As Connor turned away, he glimpsed a look of astonishment on her face, but he didn't dare stop to explain his abrupt departure. If he did, he might just pull her back into his arms and then there'd be no turning back for him. He'd be totally and irrevocably lost in something that would most likely wind up hurting both of them.

"Connor? Are you leaving?" she asked incredulously.

Unable to face her, he said in a raw, husky voice, "I have to, Jazelle. I have to go. Now!"

Not waiting to hear her response, he hurried out of the kitchen and didn't stop until he was out of the house and sitting in his truck.

The fact that his hands shook as he fastened the seat belt and started the motor caused him to mutter a few curse words under his breath. But he didn't allow himself a moment's pause to collect himself. Instead, he rapidly reversed the truck onto the road and then, without so much as a glance at Jazelle's house, gunned the vehicle in a northerly direction toward Wilhoit and home.

The next day, Jazelle was in the mudroom piling linens into the washing machine when Reeva yelled to her from somewhere in the kitchen.

"Jazelle, there's someone ringing the doorbell. Can you get it?"

She dropped what she was doing and hurried through the kitchen. "I'm on my way," she told the cook. "Probably a visitor to see Roslyn or Katherine."

"Just in time for lunch, too," Reeva said wryly. "It never fails."

Jazelle walked through the house then peeped through the door to see a deliveryman standing on the porch. A vase filled with a bouquet of beautiful, fresh-cut flowers was wedged securely in one arm. Apparently, Maureen or one of her daughters-in-law was getting flowers from the florist in town, she thought.

Promptly opening the door, she signed for the delivery. After thanking the driver, she reentered the house, carrying the bouquet.

Inside the living room, she paused long enough to glance at the card. If the flowers were going to Katherine or Roslyn, there wasn't any point in taking them out to the kitchen first. She'd carry them upstairs. If they were going to Maureen, she'd put them on the desk in her office.

But the flowers weren't for Maureen or Katherine or Roslyn. The name written across the front of the small lavender envelope read "Jazelle Hutton." What in the world? This wasn't her birthday. Not that she ever received flowers on her birthday, or any day for that matter.

Completely puzzled, she set the vase on the nearest table and quickly opened the card.

"Thank you for yesterday, Connor."

Connor had sent her flowers! After the way he'd hightailed it out of her house last night, she'd never expected to hear from him again. What did this mean? Was he trying to apologize for his abrupt departure? Or was it a custom of his to send flowers to the women he dated and dropped?

No matter the reason, she was stunned by the gesture and she read through the short message three more times before she slipped the card back into the envelope and carried the bouquet out to the kitchen.

"Who was at the door?" Reeva asked, not bothering to look around from her task of peeling boiled eggs.

"A delivery from the florist in town."

"God help us, Maureen must be expecting houseguests," Reeva said with a good-natured groan. "She normally doesn't order flowers from the florist unless something special is going on."

"Uh, these aren't for the house, Reeva." Jazelle carried them over to where the woman was working. "They're for me."

Reeva's head whipped around just as Jazelle placed the blue hobnail vase on the cabinet counter.

"Those are for you? Your daddy must be feeling as guilty as hell to make that kind of splurge. Oh, and aren't they pretty! Pink peonies, yellow daisies and blue cornflowers," she said as she touched a finger to the fragrant peony petals.

Feeling a blush on her face, Jazelle said, "They aren't from my dad, Reeva. They're from a—man."

She couldn't have stunned the cook any more if she'd yelled a warning that the ceiling was crashing down. Reeva's mouth fell open as she dropped the egg into the bowl of cold water and stepped back from the sink.

"A man?" She rested a hand on each hip as she slipped a cynical glance over Jazelle. "What are you talking about? Don't tell me that bastard who fathered Raine has come crawling back?"

Jazelle inwardly winced at the mention of Spence. As far as Reeva and the Hollisters were concerned, Spence was the dregs of society. Truth was, Jazelle considered him even lower than the manure the ranch hands wheelbarrowed out of the horse barn.

"Don't worry, Reeva. That is never going to happen. The flowers are from Connor Murphy—you know, the deputy who works with Joe. The one who came to dinner the other night."

Reeva's thin dark brows shot upward. "The deputy. Yes, I remember him. I saw him from a distance the other night, but didn't have a chance to speak with him. What's he doing sending you flowers? You must've served him a special drink or double helpings of dessert."

There wasn't any reason Jazelle should be feeling like a kid who'd stuck her finger into the sugar bowl. She was a grown, single woman. She had every right to go out with a man if she chose to. But that was just it; she'd never dated any other man until yesterday. Until Connor had looked at her with those deep blue eyes.

Folding her hands together, she said, "I, uh, didn't mention this, Reeva. Because I…well, I honestly didn't think it would amount to anything. And it hasn't. It won't. But Connor took me and Raine on a picnic yesterday. All the way to Lake Pleasant."

The suspicious look on Reeva's face deepened. "Raine went, too?"

"That's right. When I explained to Connor that I don't get to spend enough time with my son, he suggested that Raine come, too. And, actually, Reeva, Connor was great with Raine. The two of them hit it off like bread and butter."

"Hmm. And what about you and this deputy?" Reeva asked. "From the looks of these flowers, you two must have hit it off, too."

Jazelle sighed as the thrill of receiving the flowers was now giving way to reality. "Oh, I like him, Reeva. He's very enjoyable to be around. But he's not a guy a woman can take seriously. I learned my lesson with Spence. I'm not about to make the same mistake."

Reeva's doubtful expression changed to one of relief. "I guess I don't need to worry about you, then. It's just that you surprised me. You've gone all these years without a man in your life. Are you going to go out with him again?"

Jazelle picked up the flowers and carried them

over to an area of the cabinet where they wouldn't be in the way.

"I don't think so."

Reeva sniffed and went back to peeling the eggs. "Why not? Scared you might get to liking him too much?"

"Maybe. Wouldn't you be?"

"After my Dale died, I never met a man I liked that much. So I never had the chance to get scared of trying again."

Jazelle walked over to the cook and, circling an arm around her shoulders, planted a kiss on the woman's cheek. "I wish you hadn't lost the love of your life, Reeva. It isn't fair."

"Oh, honey, you know what they say, the only kind of fair in life is the kind with livestock and Ferris wheels. It just wasn't meant for me and Dale to have a long life together." She tossed the peeled egg into a plastic bowl. "Still, I can't help thinking that Liz might have turned out better if her daddy had lived. But what-ifs and maybes don't change a thing."

That's why it was best not to take chances, Jazelle thought. That's why she couldn't allow herself to make another regretful mistake. Not with Connor or any man.

Even as the warning darted through her head, her gaze fell longingly on the flowers. The beautiful bouquet symbolized everything she'd dreamed of having in her life. A man to love her. A solid marriage. A family that would never break apart.

Regret formed a painful lump in her throat and she hurried on to the laundry room before Reeva could suspect just how much Connor's bouquet had affected her.

Much later that night, sitting at a booth in the Broken Spur, Joseph's voice interrupted Connor's wandering thoughts.

"What's the matter with you, Connor? We haven't had a bite to eat in seven hours and now that you have food in front of you, you're staring into space. Are you having stomach problems?"

Pulling his gaze away from the plate-glass window that stretched across the front of the old café, Connor looked down at the platter of chili-smothered burritos and a mound of rice. Mexican food was normally his favorite, but this evening it felt like someone had tied his stomach into a row of flaming knots.

Grimacing, he whacked off a bite of the burrito with his fork. "My stomach is fine," he lied.

"Could've fooled me," Joseph replied sarcastically.

Connor forced the bite of food down his tight throat and glanced around at the late-night diners. The interior of the Broken Spur was a bit ratty with its worn flooring, scarred tabletops and ripped vinyl padding on the seats, but the food was melt-in-your-mouth delicious.

Are we gonna eat at the Broken Spur? I like

*it there, 'cause they have ice cream with brown
speckles in it.*

Raine's eager request slowly traipsed through
Connor's mind, causing what little appetite he had
to take a nosedive. Yesterday morning, before he'd
picked up Jazelle and Raine, he'd been his normal
self, Connor thought ruefully. But by the time he'd
finally gotten home last night, he'd looked in the
mirror and found himself staring back at a man he
hardly recognized.

"My stomach is okay," he repeated, then added
glumly, "It's my brain that's giving me fits."

Joseph's expression changed to one of mild concern. "What's wrong? A little too much beer on your
day off yesterday?"

Connor hadn't told Joseph about the date with
Jazelle. Mainly because he and the rest of the Hollisters were so protective of her. He figured Joseph
would've made a big deal out of handing him a long
list of do's and don'ts, along with a lecture of how
Jazelle had already endured enough heartache from
a man without Connor adding to them.

"I didn't have one beer," he admitted.

Joseph frowned. "You clearly are sick. You
should've called in this morning and stayed home."

Cursing inwardly, Connor forced himself to swallow a few bites of burrito. The chili burned all the
way down until it finally hit the pit of his hollow
stomach.

"It's not that kind of sick, Joe. To be honest, I'm

a little confused. Uh, that's not right, either. I'm a whole heck of a lot confused." Just making that much of a confession to Joseph left him drained and he wiped a weary hand over his face before he continued. "I should've never spent the day with them. It was a mistake. A huge mistake. And now I can't take any of it back."

Joseph picked up his coffee cup and took a long sip. "Them? Don't tell me you've started dating two women at a time. If that's the case, then you deserve to have a whopper of a headache and worse."

"Damn it, Joe, what do you think I am, a creep?"

"No. But you did say *them*. And *them* is plural. What am I supposed to think?"

Letting out a long breath, Connor leaned back in the seat. "I wasn't going to mention any of this, but now that I've started, I might as well finish. I figure you'll probably find out about it through Tessa anyway."

At the mention of his wife's name, Joseph leaned earnestly forward. "Tessa? What does she have to do with your brain being in a fog?"

"Nothing. But she might hear about it from Jazelle. I know the two women are friends."

Joseph was scowling now, which hardly surprised Connor. Where women were concerned, his longtime friend and partner was like a knight in shining armor, just ready and waiting to charge in and save a damsel from a villain like Connor. "Jazelle," he repeated thoughtfully. "Now I think we're getting somewhere. What have you done?"

"I haven't done anything. Except take her and Raine to the lake yesterday for a picnic. They both seemed to have a great time. There were no mishaps or problems."

Except that Connor had kept getting this soft gooey feeling in the middle of his chest throughout the day.

Joseph slanted him a guarded look. "And this has caused your brain to come unwound? I don't believe you. Something happened. And if it was bad enough to shake you up, then I hate to think how Jazelle is faring right now."

Closing his eyes, Connor massaged his burning eyelids. "Nothing earth-shattering happened," he said while mentally crossing his fingers to make up for the little white lie. No way in hell he would ever mention the kiss that he and Jazelle had shared last night in her kitchen. The whole encounter had left him feeling exposed and vulnerable and, like a coward, he'd run from her and the feelings she'd evoked in him.

"Then what's the problem?" Joseph asked.

"I can't explain, Joe. I think I've made a mistake and now I don't know what to do about it."

Joseph leaned so far over his plate, Connor expected to see the man's uniform smash into a pile of ketchup-smothered fries.

"First of all, I want to know what in heck you

were thinking? You don't date women like Jazelle. She has a child. She's a mother. A responsible one at that. She doesn't date philanderers like you. At least, I never heard of it. Until now," he added, his voice full of disapproval.

Connor blew out a heavy breath. "Everything you just said is exactly right. She's not my kind of woman. I knew that even before I asked her out. But I couldn't resist. She's just so pretty and sweet and—"

"You thought it would be fun to spend some time with her," Joseph finished with a roll of his eyes. "And now you've realized that you don't want to see her anymore and you hate telling her—because she's so nice and sweet and pretty."

Connor groaned. "You're wrong this time, Joe. I'm not worried about telling her anything like that. Frankly, she doesn't expect me to ask her for another date. She believes I only wanted a fun day with her and Raine. And she says that's the only reason she went out with me. Nothing more or less."

Joseph made a palms-up gesture. "I don't see you have a problem. If she knows it was just a casual, one-time thing then it's all over and done with. You've learned your lesson to stick with your own kind—hopefully."

The more Joseph talked, the more Connor wanted to curse. Finally, he blurted, "I sent flowers to her—out to Three Rivers. I figured that was the best place for the florist to catch up with her."

Joseph slumped back against the booth seat and

looked at him with disbelief. "Flowers? You? No. This can't be right. Your brain is in a muddle."

Using his fork, Connor absently poked a series of holes in the burrito. "Listen, Joe, I might be a little coarse, but I can be a gentleman when I try. And I wanted Jazelle to know I enjoyed her company."

"Clearly."

"Okay, so I've been stupid. I can admit that. I realize I set my sights too high. I'd never have a chance in hell with Jazelle. Not for the long haul, anyways."

A mixture of amazement and confusion skipped across Joseph's face. "You're not interested in the long haul, are you?"

Connor turned his gaze to the dusty window at the front of the café. "Where the hell do you think I'd find enough guts to do something like that? No. I'm not looking for the long haul with Jazelle, or anybody. It's just that… I really like her. I only wish… uh—" he turned a rueful look on Joseph "—that she could've been just a regular girl. You know what I'm trying to say?"

Joseph studied Connor carefully before he finally said, "Sure I do. You wish Jazelle was a girl who'd be easy to forget."

Before Joseph had married Tessa a few years ago, the man had dated only a handful of women, and that had been on an infrequent basis. Connor hadn't expected the guy to understand what was going on in his jumbled head. But somehow he'd hit the mark on the cause of Connor's mental anguish.

"Yeah. That's what I mean. After a few dates, I could move on and never look back. But I'm afraid that won't work with Jazelle."

"It won't," Joseph said bluntly. "Don't even think about trying it."

No. Connor had already decided to chalk up the day he'd spent with Jazelle and Raine as a learning experience. It was going to be damned hard to put the woman and her son out of his mind, but for their sake and his own, he'd force himself to forget them and move on.

Long moments of silence ensued as the two men focused on eating and then Joseph picked up his coffee mug and leaned back in the booth seat.

"Connor, I need to apologize to you."

Jerking his head up, Connor stared at his partner. "What?"

"You heard me," he said in a contrite voice. "I'm sorry. I've been a jerk to you. And, frankly, you should've called me out on it. Why haven't you?"

"Hell, Joe, I don't know what you're talking about. You haven't been a jerk about anything. We've been buddies since we were—what?—maybe seven or eight years old. We've always said whatever we've wanted to say to each other and never worried about it. So we're not about to start watching our words now," he said flatly.

Joseph grimaced, "That's true. But the way I've been talking, I was making it sound like you're a sorry lout or worse. I—"

"Damn it, that's stupid," Connor interjected. "I never thought for one minute that you were cutting me down."

Joseph held up his hand. "Just listen and let me explain in different terms. I've been making it sound like you're not good enough for Jazelle. And that's not true, Connor. You're a good man. If you'd change your mindset and have a little confidence in yourself, you'd be perfect for Jazelle."

Connor snorted. "What do you mean—confidence? I've never suffered from low self-esteem. Just ask a few of my old girl friends. They think 'arrogant' is my middle name."

Joseph shook his head. "You're the one who needs to be asking yourself why you're afraid to have a relationship with Jazelle. If you answer it honestly, you'll figure out what I mean."

Connor put down his fork and slumped wearily back in the seat.

Afraid of Jazelle? He wasn't afraid of her—he was downright terrified. She symbolized everything that he was not. She represented a life he'd never experienced or dreamed of having for himself.

After Connor made no attempt to reply, Joseph asked, "What are you going to do?"

It wasn't like Connor to feel lost or helpless, but this all-consuming attraction he felt for Jazelle had left him floundering.

He looked at his friend. "I wish I knew. I—"

Connor's words came to an abrupt halt as the horn

on their truck sounded from outside the café and alerted the men to an urgent radio call.

"Tell me later," Joseph said as both men quickly stood.

Pausing only long enough to throw a couple of ample bills on the checkout counter, they hurried from the café and climbed into the truck.

But even as Joseph put the truck into motion and Connor reached for the radio on the dashboard, he was thinking in the back of his mind that he couldn't give Joseph an answer as to what he was going to do about Jazelle. He couldn't even give himself an answer.

Chapter Eight

Early the next morning, Jazelle had just finished dressing for work and was about to wake Raine for breakfast when her telephone rang.

Expecting it to be Reeva, asking her to pick up something from town before she drove to the ranch, she was more than surprised when she snatched the phone off the cabinet counter and spotted Connor's name illuminated on the screen.

Her heart suddenly pounding, she leaned a hip against the cabinet just in case her legs grew too weak to support her.

"Hello, Connor."

"I apologize for calling so early, Jazelle, but I took a chance you'd be up."

"Actually, this is late for me. We had a long day yesterday and Maureen told me not to hurry in this morning. I'm still at home."

"I'm glad that I, uh, caught you before you started work."

Jazelle's mind darted in all directions as she waited for him to explain the reason for his call. When he didn't, she said, "Did you get my text message thanking you for the flowers?"

"I did. That wasn't necessary. But it was nice."

The soft tone of his voice caused something in her stomach to flip one way and then the other. "The flowers weren't necessary, either. But they were nice."

Another stretch of silence passed and then he said, "I needed to do something to make up for the way I behaved the other night—running off the way I did."

"I've already forgotten that," she assured him. She'd been too busy reliving their kiss to dwell on his abrupt departure. Besides, if he'd let that kiss of theirs go for a moment longer, she would've probably ended up in bed with the man.

He cleared his throat. "Well, I'm calling to see… if you'd like to go out again. To dinner. Just the two of us. Um…not that I don't enjoy Raine's company. But his mother deserves some grown-up time of her own, I think."

Ever since he'd hightailed it out of her house, Jazelle had wondered if he'd ever bother to ask her out again. The flowers had suggested he would, but she'd still had her doubts. Especially when it was common knowledge that he had girlfriends all over Yavapai County and beyond. Now that he'd actually extended the invitation, common sense was screaming at her to give him a firm no. But common sense couldn't extinguish the excitement and joy bubbling inside her.

"Are you sure you want to do this?" she asked.

She heard him release a long breath and then he answered, "I'm sure that I want you to say yes."

Beyond the open doorway of the kitchen, she heard Raine's bare feet patter into the bathroom. Her son was the most important thing in her life. If she thought going on a date with Connor would jeopardize his happiness, she wouldn't hesitate to end this thing with Connor here and now. But she couldn't see how eating a meal with the man could harm Raine. It wasn't like Connor was going to become a permanent fixture in their lives.

"Okay, I'll say yes. That is, if I can find a babysitter for Raine. What evening were you planning on?"

"I realize most people go out on the Friday night or the weekend," he said. "But right now my schedule has me on duty those nights. What about Thursday?"

"So far I don't think Maureen has anything major planned for that evening. Thursday should be good."

"Great. I'll pick you up about six."

"That sounds okay with me. If anything changes and I'm needed at the ranch, I'll send you a message."

"Same here," he said, adding, "Thanks, Jazelle. For saying yes."

She smiled. "Maybe you should wait to see how the evening goes before you start thanking me."

His low chuckle was like a teasing caress.

"I'll see you Thursday," he promised, then ended the connection.

"I really shouldn't do this," Jazelle said as she stood in the middle of Tessa and Joseph's living room on the Bar X. "You have your hands full with Little Joe and Spring. You don't need to take on Raine for the evening. But I'm very grateful that you offered. I don't have to tell you that asking Mom would be a last resort. And I didn't want him to have to stay late at Kiddy Korner."

From her seat on the edge of an armchair, Tessa said, "Raine isn't just spending the evening with us. He's staying the night. Did you bring everything he needed?"

Jazelle walked over and placed a backpack on a table. At the far end of the room, near the fireplace hearth, Raine and Little Joe were pushing a toy tractor back and forth between the two of them. Off to the left of the boys, Spring was attempting to comb a doll's long red hair.

"I brought extra clothing, pajamas and his toothbrush. But I honestly think I should have Connor end the evening early, so that I can come pick him up before you and Joe go to bed."

Tessa looked outraged. "Absolutely not! He'll have a wonderful time with Little Joe and Spring. You go on, enjoy a long, leisurely dinner with Connor and forget about Raine. He'll be in good hands."

Jazelle groaned. "You don't have to tell me that. But I feel like I'm taking advantage of you."

Tessa laughed. "Are you kidding? I couldn't count the times you've corralled my two little ones when we've visited Three Rivers—not to mention, Blake's twins and Chandler's two babies. You deserve a medal, Jazelle. Besides, I'd keep Raine every night of the week if I thought it would help you to have a man in your life again."

"A man in my life," Jazelle repeated wryly. "That's not going to happen, Tessa. At least, not with Connor. This date with him isn't anything like that. We're really just kind of becoming friends. He's not serious. And neither am I."

Tessa was all smiles. "It's too early for you to predict whether this will turn into something serious."

Jazelle's short laugh was cynical. "Now you're the one who must be kidding. You've known Connor for a few years now. You know exactly what he is."

Tessa's brows shot upward. "Hmm. And in your opinion, just what is he?"

Jazelle turned her gaze to the wide windows at the front of the room, but she wasn't really seeing the stand of blooming purple irises growing beyond the glass panes. She was actually seeing Connor's rugged features, tasting his lips as they'd roamed recklessly over hers.

Forcing herself to answer Tessa's question, she

said, "He's a fun, handsome guy. A responsible deputy and a devoted friend to you and Joe. Marriage material, he isn't."

"Well, maybe he's not looking to have a family right now, or even a few weeks from now. But that might eventually change. And when it does, you two might just click perfectly together. Haven't you thought about that?"

Where Connor was concerned, she'd thought about many things. The main one being that she was going to have to be very careful around the man. To let herself get emotionally or physically close to him would be like sticking her finger into a pot of boiling water and hoping the flesh wouldn't be scalded.

Purposely glancing at her watch, she said, "I'm thinking I'd better get going or I won't be ready when Connor does arrive."

After dropping a goodbye kiss on the top of Raine's head, she headed to the door with Tessa following on her heels.

"I hope you have something sexy picked out to wear," her friend said.

"My closet isn't exactly bulging with sexy clothing."

"Just make sure you don't look like an old-fashioned schoolmarm," Tessa advised.

Jazelle slanted her a clever glance. "That might be a good idea."

"Oh, Jazelle, stop it! You're a young, beautiful

woman. You need to celebrate that fact. Not run from it."

Jazelle reached for the doorknob. "Once I didn't run," she said ruefully, "and look what that got me."

"I have looked. It got you a wonderful son. You can't regret that."

Jazelle leaned over and gave Tessa a brief hug. "Thank you, my dear friend. I needed to be reminded of just how blessed I really am."

Smiling, Tessa patted her cheek then practically pushed her out the door. "Get gone. Go have a good time tonight."

If Connor had been holding on to any last-minute doubts about seeing Jazelle again, they totally vanished the moment she opened the door and invited him into the house.

Dressed in a silky blue dress and a pair of nude-colored high heels that fastened around the ankles, she looked nothing like the woman who'd stirred him up a Paloma before dinner at Three Rivers.

"Would you like to sit a few minutes before we go? Have something to drink?" she asked as she fastened a dangling pearl earring to her ear.

The majority of her hair was swept up and pinned to the crown of her head, leaving the remainder to fall in sexy disarray against her neck. A shade of rose pink dusted her cheeks, while her lips were the color of dark cherries. He didn't have to wonder if her mouth would taste as good as it looked. Ever since he'd kissed her, he'd not been able to put its sweet softness out of his mind.

Connor cleared his throat and tried not to gape at her like a besotted fool. "Thanks, but I've made reservations in Prescott. I'd hate for us to miss them."

She looked at him with surprise. "Prescott?"

"Yes. Is anything wrong with going up there?"

"Uh, no. Nothing is wrong. I, uh, just assumed we'd be dining in Wickenburg."

He smiled at her, thinking if she looked any more beautiful, he wouldn't be able to stand it.

"I thought you might enjoy seeing something different tonight."

She turned and picked up a handbag and shawl from a nearby end table. "I should've told you that I didn't need fancy. Certainly not anything that required reservations."

"You work hard taking care of the Hollisters. You deserve a bit of fancy, too," he told her.

She stepped up beside him and Connor's insides nearly wilted as her sultry scent assaulted his senses. What would she do, or think, if he pulled her into his arms and kissed her? he wondered. Would she respond as eagerly as she had a few nights ago? Or had that been one magical moment that would never happen again?

"Ready?" she asked.

"Sure. Let's go."

He placed his hand against the small of her back

and ushered her out the door before he could change his mind and pull her straight into his arms.

Minutes later, as the two of them traveled north-ward through the falling twilight, Jazelle managed to settle herself comfortably in the plush leather seat of Connor's truck, but she wasn't making any headway at calming her spinning thoughts. Not with every cell in her brain laser-focused on the man sitting next to her.

Tonight he looked like a sexy dream in dark blue jeans and a pale blue shirt that made his azure eyes even more vivid. Without his cowboy hat, his blond hair was a tousle of loose curls that fell around his ears and tickled the back of his neck. Each time she looked at him, the more she realized what a fool she'd been for thinking a dinner date with Connor could be casual.

From the moment he'd helped her into the truck and taken his seat behind the steering wheel, she'd wondered if something had happened with the ve-hicle's electrical wiring. The air inside the cab had felt so charged, she'd half expected to see smoke drift out of the air-conditioning vents.

Silly. The only thing that's about to ignite inside this truck is you, Jazelle. One look at Connor's rug-ged face and all you've been able to think about is having the man kiss you again, of feeling his hard, strong arms wrapped around you. Do you honestly think you can keep your distance from him when every part of you wants to get closer?

"Would you like for me to turn the air-conditioning to a warmer setting?"

Her churning thoughts were interrupted by his question and she suddenly realized she'd unwittingly wrapped her arms around herself as though she was freezing. Thank goodness he didn't know that thoughts of him had brought on the shiver, not the cool air blowing from the dash vents.

"I'm okay." She gestured to the interior of the cab. "You have a nice truck. I'm sure you've noticed that mine is heading toward antique age. But it's still going strong and since I have to drive back and forth over very rough roads to work every day, it works for me."

He cast her a curious glance. "Is working for the Hollisters something you always plan to do?"

She'd not expected him to be interested in her future plans. All along she'd been trying to convince herself that, other than his work as a deputy, he didn't have a serious bone in his body. Now she was wondering if she'd been cutting him short.

Squaring around in the seat so that she was facing him, she said, "When I first graduated high school, I was saving up and making plans to go to college. I wanted a degree in mine engineering. My dad works in mining and there're plenty of those type jobs in the state. But…" She paused and sighed. "All of those plans came to a halt when I became pregnant with

Raine. After that, I've had to focus on making a living for the two of us."

Several seconds ticked before he finally said, "I'm assuming Raine's father never offered any monetary help to raise his son."

Her cynical snort sounded awful, but she couldn't help it. The idea of Spence taking any kind of responsibility for the child he'd helped to conceive was ludicrous.

"No. That never happened," she said and shrugged. "I probably wouldn't have accepted it anyway. It would've felt like dirty money—from a thief. You know what I mean?"

"Unfortunately, I do. When you know something is given grudgingly, it changes everything."

She thoughtfully studied his profile. In many ways, he'd been like her. Left without family support at a very young age. He understood what it was like to have to scrap for himself. "I think you really do understand."

He grunted. "Sure, I do. After Dad died, my uncles did a good job of teaching me all about selfishness and what it meant to be tolerated rather than loved. Uncle Felton especially despised me. He only let me stay at his place because he didn't want all his friends to view him as a jackass. Funny thing, though, when he died, he willed part of his estate to me. Not that it amounted to much, but in the end, he thought about me. Guess his conscience got to bothering him."

"Did you accept the money, or whatever it was?"

"It was a bit of money and two vehicles. I donated all of it to my grandmother's church. She wasn't alive to see my contribution, but I knew she'd be happy with me, and that's all that mattered."

Pride tempered by generosity and sentimentality, Jazelle thought. What else was she going to learn about the man before the night was over?

"My mother has already made it clear that she's not leaving me anything whenever she dies," she said with a nonchalant lift of her shoulders. "But that's perfectly okay with me."

"What's she going to do? Leave whatever she has to Raine?"

"Oh my, no! She doesn't view him as her grand-child. She's sees him as an illegitimate mistake, one created by her loose daughter."

He scowled. "That's pretty harsh, Jazelle."

"Well, in her mind, she has more reason than that to cut me out. She's never forgiven me for wanting to go live with my father. I don't expect she ever will." Pausing, she shook her head. "Actually, she might forgive me if I went to her and groveled... But everything about that would be phony. I don't need that kind of conditional love."

Nodding, he said, "So back to your idea of college, are you still holding on to that plan?"

"For a long time I debated about doing online classes. That's how Tag's wife, Emily-Ann, is getting her nursing degree and she's close to being finished. But to be honest, I don't want to leave Three Rivers for another job. It's become my home and the Hollisters are my family. I don't want to move away from them. I suppose that sounds like I don't have any goals for myself. But I like being a part of what makes Three Rivers the great ranch that it is and I'm happy there. That counts for something, doesn't it?"

He turned his head just enough for her to see a wide smile on his face and then he reached over and clasped his hand around hers. "Happy. Yeah. I'd say that counts for everything."

His touch caused her heart to leap into a joyous thump and she realized that, no matter what happened in the future, she was glad she was here with him tonight.

In Prescott, they had dinner at a small but highly recommended Italian restaurant that put more emphasis on the quality of its food than the ambience of the interior. Jazelle had appeared delighted by his choice of dining places and, all through the meal, she'd exclaimed how delicious everything tasted.

Connor had been expecting Jazelle to focus most of their dinner conversation on Raine, or at least, express a concern about being away from him for the evening, but she didn't. Instead, she seemed perfectly happy to focus her attention on him, which was an unfamiliar situation for Connor. Until Jazelle, he'd never had a woman ask him questions that actually required him to think about himself and his life.

By the time they'd ended the meal with dessert and strong cups of espresso, Connor realized he didn't want the evening to end. He wanted to take Jazelle to some quiet club where they could slow dance in the dark and he could pretend that she belonged to him. Not just for the night, but forever.

The thought had come at him out of nowhere and he'd been so shaken by it, he'd hustled her out of the restaurant and headed the truck straight back to Wickenburg.

"You didn't mention who's watching Raine tonight," he told her as he neared the turnoff to the country road that led to her house. "I'd be happy to take you wherever to pick him up."

"Thanks for offering, but that won't be necessary. He's staying overnight with Tessa and Joe. I'll be picking him up on my way to the ranch in the morning."

"Oh. I thought—that's why I didn't offer to go anywhere else after dinner," he said, thinking that was partially the truth. "I figured you would need to pick Raine up before it got too late."

From the corner of his eye, he saw her shake her head. "I'm sorry. I should've explained the situation." She looked at him then let out a soft laugh. "I thought you left Prescott early because you were getting tired of my company."

"No," he said and then chuckled. "I'll bet Joe and Tessa are having a high old time entertaining three kids."

Her groan was full of misgivings. "Don't make me feel any worse than I already do. The only reason I agreed to let Tessa babysit Raine in the first place was that she kept insisting. Honestly, though, he's pretty obedient for Tessa, and he and Little Joe get along great."

When Connor didn't make any sort of reply, she turned slightly in the seat and looked at him. "I imagine you already know that Tessa and Joe are trying for a third child."

Stunned by this news, he glanced at her. "Another baby? No! I didn't know. Joe doesn't talk about such things to me."

She pressed fingertips to her lips. "Oops. I just assumed. Please don't mention to Joe that I said anything. Tessa and I were just having girl talk and… well, I expect he'll tell you whenever it does happen."

He whistled under his breath. "A third baby. Spring is just now getting good at walking and talking. I can't imagine taking on another one. And so quickly."

"No. I don't expect you can imagine having that many children for yourself. But Tessa and Joe are perfect together and they know how they want to build their future. I wouldn't be surprised if they had six children before it's all said and done."

"Well, if anybody can handle being the father of six, it's Joe," he replied.

If you'd change your mindset and have a little confidence in yourself, you'd be perfect for Jazelle.

From out of nowhere, Joseph's words drifted through his mind. How could his partner picture Connor as being perfect for Jazelle? In many ways, she was like Tessa. She was meant to be a wife and mother. She was meant to be loved and cherished. Not enjoyed for a few weeks then tossed away like Raine's father had tossed her away.

So why did you ask the woman out again, Connor? Why didn't you just move on to someone else, to a woman who'd be perfectly content with a night or two of hot sex?

Maybe because he was tired of moving on. Connor attempted to answer the questions darting around in his head. Maybe because he was bored with those kinds of shallow women. Most of all, he might be sick of being truly alone.

He was still deep in thought when the truck topped a rise and Jazelle's mailbox appeared in the glow of the headlights. He parked in the driveway next to her house and shut off the engine.

She said, "I can't believe the trip back is already over. You will come in, won't you? *I'll* make coffee this time. You can even have a second dessert, if you like. I brought home bread pudding that Reeva made for dinner tonight."

Coffee, dessert and Jazelle. How was he supposed to survive that kind of temptation? All through dinner, he'd struggled to keep his gaze anywhere other than her plush lips, creamy skin and the curves pushing at the fabric of her blue dress. He'd tried not to imagine himself making love to her, but he'd failed miserably.

He turned to look at her. "I don't think I should," he said honestly.

The warm smile she gave him very nearly caused Connor to groan out loud.

"Why?" she asked. "Worried about getting a belly? Or are you tired of listening to my chatter?"

Something pierced him right in the middle of his chest and before he could figure out what was happening to him, he leaned across the console and cupped her cheek in the palm of his hand.

"I'm not tired of your chatter or anything else about you," he said gently. "But I am tired of waiting—to do this again."

A question flashed in her eyes, followed by the sudden dawning of what he was about to do.

"Connor."

His whispered name was more like a plea and the sound of longing filled him with the need to give instead of take, to cherish rather than use. What did that mean?

Before he could answer the self-directed question, Jazelle suddenly closed the tiny space between their faces and planted her lips on his. The contact was all it took to push everything from his mind and, for the next few seconds, he let the exquisite pleasure of her kiss wash over him.

When she finally pulled away, she gazed at him with eyes that were warm and smiling.

"You know," she said softly, "I was getting pretty tired of waiting on you to do that."

His heart thumped hard against his chest. "I wasn't sure. I thought—"

She placed a finger on his lips. "You're thinking too much—about everything. And so am I."

He sucked in a deep breath, but it felt like his lungs were still starved for oxygen.

"When did you decide that?" he asked, his voice so husky he hardly recognized it.

"I'm not sure." An impish smile tilted the corners of her lips. "Probably somewhere between the salad and the ravioli."

She was right, he decided. From the moment he'd met this woman, he'd done more contemplating and overanalyzing than he'd done in his entire life. And frankly, it was making him crazy.

"I guess I have been weighing things an awful lot," he admitted.

Her hand found his and gently squeezed. "Come on, Deputy Murphy. Let's go in. I'm not going to hurt you."

Even though she was teasing, Connor was imagining tiny pieces of his heart scattered through the rooms of Jazelle's house. And the notion brought him up short. His heart? What the heck was wrong with him? That was the last part of his body he should be worried about right now.

Grinning back at her, he said, "Okay. You don't have to twist my arm any harder."

She laughed and in that moment Connor realized Jazelle was swiftly and surely changing his life. And even worse, he couldn't find the will to stop her.

Chapter Nine

Once they entered the house, Jazelle didn't bother to switch on a lamp in the living room. Instead, she looped her arm around his and guided him on to the kitchen where a night-light illuminated a portion of the cabinets and the cookstove.

Dropping her hold, she left him standing in the middle of the room and walked over to the stove to turn on the light beneath the vent.

"The only other time Raine spent the night away from me was when I had a bad case of the flu. Reeva kept him at her place for a couple of nights," she said. "I felt too awful then to notice how quiet the house was without him, but I'm noticing now."

Connor stood where he was and fought the urge to

go to her, to put his arms around her and to tell her to forget the coffee, forget everything but the two of them being together.

He breathed deeply then said, "I imagine right about now he and Little Joe have played themselves to sleep."

She glanced at a wall clock hanging near the kitchen table. "Probably," she agreed. "Tessa is a stickler about putting the kids to bed at the same time every night."

"You're not worried about Raine, are you?"

"No." She opened a cabinet door and pulled down a can of coffee. "I try not to be one of those mothers who constantly frets and obsesses over her child. But sometimes it's hard not to worry."

"That's understandable." The dim lighting was just enough to illuminate her golden hair and the alluring shape of her body beneath the blue dress. She was the most feminine woman he'd ever met and the sweet softness of her pulled on him like nothing ever had before.

"Whenever I have to work late at night, I take him to the ranch with me. There's always someone there to help keep an eye on him. I've never left him with a sitter to go on a date." She paused from spooning coffee into a filtered basket to glance over her shoulder at him. "But like I told you, since Spence, you're the only man I've gone out with."

The night Connor had dinner with the Hollisters at Three Rivers, Jazelle had told him that she didn't date. And even before then, Joseph had admitted he'd not known of her having a boyfriend. Still, Connor hadn't taken the information literally. Frankly, he'd not been able to believe a woman who looked like Jazelle could live such a solitary life for that length of time. But now that he'd come to know Jazelle, he did believe it. And the fact that he was the first man she'd trusted enough to go out with since Raine's father, left him feeling very humbled.

His gaze locked with hers and he closed the short distance between them to place his hands upon her shoulders. "Why did you choose me, Jazelle? Because you think I'm not serious and that makes you feel safe?"

Her lips parted as though the questions surprised her and then she shook her head. "If you want to know the truth, Connor, I've never felt safe around you. I don't feel safe at this very moment. But that hasn't stopped me from wanting you."

Her last words were like a punch in the gut and, before he realized what he was doing, he pulled her into his arms and pressed his cheek against the top of her head. She felt incredibly warm against him and the scent of flowers drifted up from her hair. Just having her this close played havoc with his senses.

"I've wanted you from the time I first laid eyes on you," he admitted. "And ever since then I've been trying to convince myself that I'm not the right man for you. That for both our sakes, I need to walk away."

Tilting her head back, her eyes delved into his. "And now?"

He gently touched her cheek and marveled at the softness beneath his fingertips. "I think we need to forget the coffee. Don't you?"

Her answer was to rise up on the tips of her toes and angle her mouth over his.

The instant their lips meshed, Connor's arms tightened around her then lifted her, until her feet were completely off the floor and her hands were gripping his shoulders.

He kissed her that way until his arms began to ache from the effort. After he set her back on the floor, she turned away from him long enough to fasten the lid on the coffee can. Then, without a single word passing between them, she gathered his hand in hers and led him out of the kitchen and down the short hall until they reached the open doorway of her bedroom.

There was no night-light to show a path, but there was enough moonlight filtering through the windows to illuminate a standard-size four-poster. A patchwork quilt served as a spread, while the pillows were covered with ruffle-edged shams. The simple sight reminded him of everything his home wasn't and, for one split second, the thought of turning and running for a second time dashed through his head.

But then her warm hand tugged him further into the room and suddenly it didn't matter if he was all wrong for her, or if she was going to tear his heart into a thousand pieces. All that mattered was that she wanted him and he wanted her. The rest he'd deal with later. Much later.

Once Jazelle had him standing beside the bed, she immediately reached for the buttons on his shirt and very nearly laughed at her boldness and the way her hands shook as she tried to part the fabric away from his chest.

"You'll have to forgive me, Connor. I'm pretty rusty at all of this," she told him.

He caught her hands between his and lifted them to his lips. Kissing the knuckles of her fingers, he said, "You're doing everything right."

She searched his handsome face for a sign that he was impatient, or even amused by her clumsy efforts, but there was nothing like that to be found in his expression. Rather, she saw a gentle desire that pierced the very core of her heart.

"I was a teenager the last time this happened," she admitted, her voice straining to get past the lump of emotion in her throat. "Since then I've not learned anything about making love. Will you show me?"

An anguished look crossed his face and then his head was close to hers, his lips nuzzling her ear. "Oh, Jazelle, just kiss me, touch me—any way you want. The rest will take care of itself." Sliding his forefinger beneath her chin, he lifted her face toward his. "Okay?"

Smiling, she pushed her hands up his chest and

then linked them at the back of his neck. "Very okay," she whispered.

Groaning, he closed the gap between their faces and captured her lips with his. Jazelle gave herself up to the magical taste of his kiss and, for the next few moments, let her mind drift as his hands roamed up and down her back, down to her buttocks, then up to where the zipper of her dress fastened between her shoulder blades.

With his lips still feasting on hers, he slowly lowered the zipper until the bodice of her dress loosened and fell down around her hips. Instantly, his hands were on her lace covered breasts, kneading and cupping their fullness until the nipples turned to throbbing buds.

Moaning deep in her throat, she desperately pushed her tongue against his teeth, while at the same time arching the lower part of her body into his. With no hesitation, he allowed her passage into the intimate cave of his mouth and Jazelle's senses spun wildly as she explored the ribbed roof and sharp edges of his teeth. The faint taste of espresso lingered on his tongue, along with some other delicious flavor that belonged uniquely to him.

In the back of her mind, she realized if she kissed him for the rest of her life it wouldn't be enough. If he held her this tightly for days on end, she would still long to be wrapped in his arms.

By the time he lifted his head and dropped his lips to the cleavage spilling over the cups of her bra,

Jazelle was lost in a firestorm of sensations. Streaks of hot pleasure raced through her as the tip of his tongue made lazy circles upon the plump flesh.

Eventually, he pulled back just long enough to undo the clasp of her bra. As soon as the pink lacy garment fell to the floor, his mouth returned to her breasts and for long, long moments, he tormented each nipple with sweet kisses and taunting little nibbles.

The ache between her thighs intensified with each passing second, until desire was gripping her body, begging her to draw closer to the cause of her agony. He must have recognized her desperation because he finally pulled back and removed the last of her clothing.

After he lifted her onto the bed, he rapidly stripped down to his boxers and then stretched out next to her on the smooth quilt.

A sigh slipped past her lips as he gathered her into his arms and rested his forehead against hers.

"I hadn't planned on this happening tonight," he whispered, using his fingers to comb fallen strands of hair from her face. "To be honest, I wasn't expecting it to ever happen, but subconsciously I suppose I was hoping it would. That's why I've been carrying protection around in my wallet."

With the front of her body pressed against his, the heat of his flesh was spreading through her like the blistering afternoon sun. It melted her very bones and caused drops of perspiration to emerge above her upper lip.

"Hoping. I've been doing a bit of that, too," she admitted. "I wasn't sure you wanted me *this* much. And I've been telling myself I shouldn't get this close to you."

Touching a finger to her swollen lips, his eyes roamed her face. "And now? Are you sure about this—us?"

Her throat aching with unbidden emotion, she cupped a hand against the side of his face. "I'm sure that I want you next to me. Inside me. And just to ease your mind, Connor, I don't have any strings hidden in this bed. I threw them all away."

"Damn it, Jazelle," he whispered against her cheek. "I'm not worried about strings. I only want to make you happy."

Happy? Yes, she thought. He'd already done that just by walking into her life and reminding her that she was a desirable woman, a woman who deserved to feel the joy of having a man make love to her.

"Having you here—next to me—is making me happy, Connor."

He looked at her for long moments and then with a needy groan, his lips came down on hers.

The kiss started out softly but swiftly developed into a wild, reckless connection that left Jazelle panting and Connor sitting up on the side of the bed and reaching for his jeans.

Through a foggy haze of desire, she recognized

he was searching through his wallet for a condom. She started to tell him that she was protected by the Pill and that for the past few years she'd taken the medication to keep her cycles regular. But just as quickly she decided to keep the information to herself. If by some wild chance she got pregnant, she didn't want him thinking it was because her birth control had failed.

When he returned to the middle of the mattress, he wasted no time in positioning himself over her. Relieved that he wasn't going to make her wait any longer, Jazelle wrapped her arms around him. With their gazes locked, he lowered his hips and slowly entered her until they were totally and completely one.

Sparks of pleasure showered through her body, momentarily stunning her senses. Then he gently whispered her name and the sound of his voice pulled her focus to his face. Through a haze of desire, she saw tenderness in his eyes and it flooded her heart with emotions she'd never felt before.

"Connor. Oh, Connor."

Groaning, he bent his head to hers and pressed his lips against her damp forehead.

"Yes, my sweet," he whispered. "We're together—finally."

The emotion in his voice shook her and she closed her eyes and tried not to wonder what it meant, or to let herself believe his words were coming from his heart. No. All she wanted was to feel the pleasure of his body and hope that she could give him the same in return.

With her hands gripping his back, she arched her hips upward and somehow managed to draw him even deeper into her.

He growled with pleasure and began to move, slowly at first then faster and faster. Jazelle matched her movements to his until his hard, driving thrusts carried her to a place where there was only him and her, the silver moonlight bathing their bodies, their heartbeats merging, pounding out a rhythm that felt so very much like love.

Beneath her hands, his flesh was hard and hot. Under her lips, his skin tasted rich and salty, and so very masculine. She wanted to cover him in kisses, touch him anywhere and everywhere, until each hard contour of his body was imprinted in her brain.

Beyond the boundless pleasures he was bestowing upon her body, her mind registered that she was on a journey that was taking every thought, every hope and dream she'd ever possessed, and sending it down a totally different path. And the shocking reality was that she didn't want to change course. Not tonight.

The only thing that mattered was having Connor inside her and finding some sort of relief for the pressure that threatened to split her right down the middle.

She was desperately twisting and turning beneath him, whimpering with unbearable need, when his lips suddenly found hers. The hungry kiss caused a wall inside her to collapse and suddenly she felt her whole being tumbling end-over-end, free falling into a velvety night sky.

When Connor finally became aware of his surroundings, he realized the side of his face was pressed into Jazelle's shoulder and a portion of her hair rested across his closed eyes. Beneath his chest, he could feel her breasts rising and falling as she struggled to regain her breath.

Slowly, he rolled his weight off her and, with his back flat against the mattress, he stared at the dark ceiling and attempted to gather what was left of his rattled senses.

Something had to be physically wrong with him, Connor decided. His head was still spinning and he wasn't sure if his lungs would ever work at full capacity again. And if those maladies weren't enough to trouble him, there was something strange going on in the middle of his chest, like a sweet ache that wouldn't go away.

This wasn't the way a man was supposed to feel after he'd had sex with a woman, Connor mentally argued. Instead of reaching for his clothes, he wanted to reach for her. Again. Damn it, was age catching up with him already? Or was Jazelle too much woman for him?

Moaning softly, she rolled toward him and rested her hand on his arm. Thankfully the touch of her fingers was all it took to calm the upheaval in his head, and he smiled at her as he lifted the palm of her hand to his lips.

"You look very beautiful right now," he murmured.

She smiled back at him. "I'm sweaty, my hair is all tangled, and I'm sure you've kissed away every last bit of my lipstick."

She didn't need makeup and smooth hair to make her beautiful, he thought. Her beauty came from deep inside her. It glowed in her brown eyes and filled her smiles. Each time she touched him, he felt the loveliness radiating within her. Maybe that's why a part of him had always been scared to get close to her. Maybe that's why now, at this very moment, he wanted to pull her into his arms and swear that he would never let her go.

"And it tasted mighty good, too," he said, doing his best to keep his voice light.

She scooted closer and as she wrapped her arm around his waist, the tips of her breasts pressed into his chest. Desire flickered in his loins and he wondered if a second round of lovemaking with her might actually kill him.

Lovemaking. No. That wasn't what the two of them had been doing, he mentally argued. What they'd just shared was good, hot sex. Nothing more. Nothing less. After a second time, he'd realize there was nothing special about the way she made him feel. It was all chemistry and nothing about love.

"Are you sorry you let me drag you into the house?" she asked.

Amusement arched his brows. "Drag? It was more like I willingly let you lead me."

She chuckled. "Okay. So you did."

Planting a hand against the small of her back, he snuggled her body closer to his. "For a second or two, I considered running. But I'm glad I didn't."

The teasing expression on her face instantly sobered. "Really, Connor? You don't regret this?" she asked.

The soft, achy feeling in his chest suddenly worsened, but he was determined to ignore it. "How could I? Right here is where I want to be."

She didn't look a bit convinced. "You, uh…" She closed her eyes as her forefinger drew an abstract design upon his shoulder. "Well, let's be honest, Connor, you don't need me for sex."

She was right, he didn't. He needed her for a thousand reasons other than physical gratification. But to tell her such a thing would make it sound like he was falling in love with her. And that would be misleading. Because he wasn't falling for her. He was simply enjoying her.

"You don't need me for sex, either," he said pointedly. "I think we're here in your bed because we honestly like each other. And that's even a better reason, isn't it?"

She opened her eyes and he was relieved to see the brown orbs were soft and warm and totally inviting.

"Much better." She squirmed until her lips were hovering close to his. "The coffee and bread pudding are still waiting in the kitchen."

"Mmm. Remind me again around midnight—or later," he said and then muffled her laugh with a kiss.

"Are you asleep over there?"

Connor glanced away from the computer screen and over to Joseph, who was sitting at his desk, his chin propped on the heel of his hand. Their shift had ended more than an hour ago, but both men had chosen to stay to do what digging they could toward solving Joel's cause of death.

So far, they'd located two cattle haulers Joel sometimes hired whenever he'd purchased something from the sale ring. Unfortunately, neither man had been able to supply any helpful information.

Connor said, "I'm not sleeping. I'm thinking."

Grunting, Joseph said, "That's a scary thought. When you think, it always means trouble."

No one knew that better than Connor himself. Two days had passed since he'd spent three-fourths of the night in Jazelle's bed and ever since then he'd not been able to shut off the memories. She'd made love to him with a passion that had stunned him. Now all he wanted was to have her back in his arms, his lips on hers, their bodies connected.

Clearing his throat, he tried to shake the erotic thoughts away and focus his attention on Joseph. "Yeah, but sometimes trouble is needed to get things rolling. And that's what we need right now, Joe, to get your father's case steamrolling forward."

"True." Joseph wiped a hand over his face. "Yesterday, Tag and I searched more area north of the well pump."

"Did you find anything?"

"No. And I've decided it's time to end those rides. We have those few scraps of Dad's shirt and his spur rowel. And we know exactly where they were located. That's enough to give us an idea of Dad's location when he died. Besides, it always makes me damned depressed to ride over that particular part of the ranch and think about what he must've gone through."

"I agree with you, Joe. To make any progress, we have to locate the woman your father was seeing at the sale barn. And I think I have an idea of how to do it."

Joseph merely looked at him. Years of searching with little results had tempered the man's hope for uncovering the truth of the incident.

"Tell me," he said.

Connor swiveled his chair so that he was facing his partner. "We need to visit the stockyards at Phoenix and ask questions."

Joseph let out a tired groan. "Connor, what the hell do you think Uncle Gil has been doing? He's already made several trips down there and struck out."

"I know that! But the stockyards has to be our

starting point. And this time, you and I are going to take flyers and pass them out."

Joseph frowned at him. "Flyers? What's going to be on these flyers? We're searching for a blond-haired woman who might've had an affair with Joel Hollister?" he asked sarcastically.

"Damn, Joe. What's the matter with you? You don't think that about your father."

Joseph's shoulders slumped against the back of the desk chair. "No. Not for one second have I ever believed Dad was unfaithful to Mom. I'm just damned tired of not knowing—of getting nowhere with this."

Rising from his seat, Connor walked over and rested a hip on the corner of Joseph's desk. "Listen, I think we need to treat this like a missing person case. Right now, our main focus is to find a certain woman. So we'll put a picture of your dad on the flyer and the time period he attended the auctions, along with inquiries about the unidentified woman. If the right person sees it and puts two and two together, we might just get a lead."

Joseph thoughtfully weighed Connor's suggestion. "A missing person case, huh? Buddy of mine, you might just be on to something. Find her and we'll find some answers."

Connor grinned. "That's the way I see it."

"When can we go?" Joseph directed the question to himself as much as to Connor. "Sales only happen on Wednesday and Saturday. Otherwise, the only people around the barns would be the workers."

"Hmm. We definitely need to go when the auction is taking place," Connor agreed. "And we need to get the flyers made up. Next Wednesday is probably the soonest we could go. We have that day off, but not Saturday."

Joseph sighed. "Yeah, I looked at our schedule this morning. What about you? Do you have anything planned for Wednesday?"

For the past two days, Connor's plans had revolved around seeing Jazelle again—anytime or anywhere he could manage. But, so far, both of them had been tied up with work.

"No. I can go Wednesday," he said.

There must've been a hint of reluctance in his voice because Joseph shot him a meaningful look. "You did have something planned, but you don't want to disappoint me."

"Hell, Joe, I said no. We're going on Wednesday. It's settled."

Joseph crossed his arms across his chest. "You're thinking you wanted to save that day for Jazelle. Right?"

Connor wasn't going to lie to his friend. "I was. But I have no idea what Jazelle might be doing that day. And, anyway, she'd understand about this thing with Joel's investigation. She wants the mystery solved just as much as anyone in your family wants it."

Joseph left the desk chair and walked over to the coffeepot. As he filled a foam cup, he said, "Jazelle came to work at the ranch probably about a year after Dad died. She never got the chance to meet him, but she's heard plenty of stories about him."

Connor thoughtfully watched Joseph stir powdered creamer into the drink. "Jazelle hasn't had much of a father figure in her life. She told me she was thirteen when her father left the family. She defends his reasons for divorcing her mother. Still, I can tell she feels he deserted her."

"One time I walked into the kitchen at Three Rivers and heard Reeva cursing the man up one side and down the other."

Connor stared at him. "Sherman Hutton was at Three Rivers?"

"No. That was the reason Reeva was cursing the man. She was fighting mad because it was Jazelle's twenty-first birthday and Mom was throwing a party for her. The man didn't bother to show up or even call his daughter to wish her a happy day. To some folks, I guess that's trivial stuff, but Reeva told me that Jazelle had gone upstairs crying. I think a few days later, he called and apologized for missing her birthday, but I figure the apology was too little, too late."

Jazelle crying. Just the thought of it tore at Connor. If he ever met Sherman Hutton personally, he'd have a hard time keeping his hands from wrapping around the man's neck. "What a bastard," he stated.

Joseph sank into the chair at his desk. "You know, Connor, I used to feel sorry for myself because I lost Dad. He was still a young man and I expected to have him around for a long time. But when I think about Jazelle's broken family, then you never having a mother and losing your father…well, I see now just how blessed I've been."

Connor pushed his hip off Joseph's desk and ambled restlessly around the small office. "I tell you what I think, Joe. Raine needs a daddy like Little Joe and Spring have. The boy needs that more than anything."

"I'll tell you what I was thinking the other night when Tessa and I babysat Raine. I was thinking the boy needs *you* for a daddy. And, frankly, you need him."

Connor let out a cynical snort. "You're losing it, Joe! You want the kid's life ruined? A man has to know how to comfort and nurture. He has to know when to use a firm hand or a soft one. He needs to understand when he's spoiling a child too much, or not enough. And that's only a part of being a dad." Pausing, he shook his head. "I don't have that in me, Joe."

"You'd be surprised what you have in you if you'd just bother to look." Joseph sipped his coffee before adding, "Raine carries the arrowhead in his pocket all the time. He told Tessa the piece of flint was going to bring him a daddy."

Oh, God. Oh, no. He couldn't allow the child to hang his hopes on him, Connor thought. No more than he could let Jazelle start believing their relationship was a long-term thing.

Swallowing hard, he said, "Wonder where the boy got that idea? I certainly didn't give it to him. And I don't believe Jazelle would suggest such a thing to her son."

"Connor, children get ideas on their own."

Shaking his head, Connor walked to the opposite side of the room and stared unseeingly at the huge map of Yavapai County hanging on the wall.

"I wish you hadn't brought any of this up, Joe. I was having a good day until you ruined it with all this family talk."

"Well, pardon me," Joseph muttered. "I've been getting the impression that you're getting serious about Jazelle."

"I don't know why. I've only dated her twice." Even to Connor's own ears that sounded stupid. So much had been packed into those hours he'd spent with Jazelle. He already knew how it felt to hold her in his arms, to taste the sweetness on her lips and hear her soft whispers in his ear.

Joseph chuckled. "Once is all it takes. I've told you before how I took one look at Tessa and flipped for her."

"Well, I don't think I've flipped for Jazelle. We're just…enjoying each other's company, that's all."

Joseph was raking him with a dubious look when Connor's phone dinged with the notification of a new message.

He went to his desk to check the phone and was

totally surprised to see Jazelle had sent him a text message.

I don't know if you're anywhere near my house or whether you're on duty, but I'm bringing a basket full of food from the ranch home with me. Raine and I would love for you to have dinner with us. If you're able, please let me know. XO

Frowning, he looked over at Joseph. "What does it mean when a message is signed off with an XO?"

Joseph laughed. "You, the playboy of Yavapai County, don't know what that means? I take everything back I've ever said about your womanizing. You need to get out more."

Pulling a smirk at him, Connor said, "Well, I should've kept my damned mouth shut and just tried to figure it out myself."

Chuckling to himself, Joseph stood and walked over to where Connor was still holding the phone. "Who's that from, anyway? Not from the sheriff, I'm assuming. Our boss wouldn't be sending you love and hugs and kisses."

Connor's eyes widened on his friend's face. "That's what it means? Really?"

"Yes, really. Now, who's it from? The little black-haired waitress from Congress?"

"Julie?" He snorted a laugh. "The only thing she wants to give me is a hard slap across the face. Uh, this is Jazelle. She's invited me to have dinner at her place. I don't know what to tell her. We're off duty, but still on call. As soon as I get my plate filled, I might have to jump up and leave."

"If you do, Jazelle will understand." Joseph reached over and gave Connor's shoulder an affectionate shake. "Tell her you'll be there. That's what you really want to do, isn't it?"

There was no point in lying to himself or Joseph. He wanted to be with Jazelle again. No matter the circumstances.

"It is." He pulled the phone closer and rapidly typed a reply.

I'll be there at 6:30.

He slipped the phone into his shirt pocket then, in afterthought, pulled it out and added an XO at the end of his message.

Seeing Joseph was grinning at him like a Cheshire cat, Connor explained, "That might get me an extra helping on my plate."

"Sure, Connor," Joseph said dryly. "I'm positive an extra helping of food is the only thing on your mind."

At this moment, Connor would hate for his partner to read the erotic thoughts parading through his mind. "Don't worry. Raine makes a great chaperone."

Joseph snickered, but Connor didn't laugh along with him. Not when every cell in his body was aching to make love to Jazelle again.

Chapter Ten

"Mommy, why do I have to take a bath now? I might get dirty again before bedtime and then you'll make me wash all over again."

"You're not going to take a bath," Jazelle corrected her son. "You're going to take a shower. A quick one, at that. Now jump in there and get to scrubbing. Connor will be here before you get dressed."

She handed Raine a washcloth and a bar of soap, then positioned him beneath the spray of warm water. "You and Nick must have rolled in the dirt down at the horse barn. You have it all over you."

As the boy began to wash his face, trails of muddy water raced down his chest. "Nick was pulling me in a Radio Flyer. That's a wagon. Did you know that,

Mommy? And we went so fast that dust was going all on me. It was super fun!"

Thank God for Blake's teenage son, Jazelle thought. Having a little twin sister and brother, he was excellent at corralling young kids and keeping them happy at the same time. She'd had a very busy day at Three Rivers serving a huge lunch to a group of cattle buyers. All throughout the event, she'd not had to worry about what Raine might be getting into.

"I'm sure it was," Jazelle replied. "And now you're going to get to see Connor again. You're having a fun day all around, aren't you?"

"I sure am!" He squinted at her through a face full of soap bubbles. "Is Connor going to be wearing his badge? He might let me touch it. Do you think he will?"

"If you ask him nicely, he probably will. But he might not be wearing his badge. You'll just have to wait and see," she told her son, while wondering how one afternoon with the man had been enough for Raine to form such a deep bond with the man.

Jazelle, forget about the quick bond Raine has made with Connor. You jumped into bed with the man at the end of your second date! He's probably already labeled you as fast and loose—just like the other women who've walked in and out of his life.

Trying not to let that miserable thought drag down her high spirits, she grabbed a bottle of shampoo and squirted a small amount on the top of Raine's head. "Wash that out of your hair and rinse off."

"Then I can get out of here?" he asked, as though the last couple of minutes had been enough torture.

"Yes, you may. And after you dry off, put on the clothes that I've laid on your bed."

She left him to finish the shower and hurried out to tidy the living room. Her little house didn't have a dining room, but she took pains in setting the kitchen table with her best dishes, then went to her bedroom to change into a fresh dress.

She was attaching a pair of silver hoops to her ears when Raine came racing into the room.

"I'm all ready," he announced as he came to a screeching halt on the toes of his sneakers.

From her view in the mirror, she noticed he'd made an effort to brush his hair, but part of the crown was a lopsided lump.

"You look very handsome," she told him.

Grinning, he held out his palm for her to see. "I have my arrowhead, too. I showed it to Nick and he said it's a mighty fine one! So I got to tell Connor. Do you think we could go hunt for more arrowheads, Mommy? If you ask him, he might take us there again."

The eager excitement on her son's face was a precious sight, but it also sent a prick of unease through her. Should she sit her son down and try to explain that Connor was just a friend, who might not always be around?

Ever since she and Connor had taken their relationship to a deeper level, the question had been on

Jazelle's mind. But then, she'd continued to tell herself that Raine was too young to understand.

"I think it might be better if you ask him yourself." The child would be putting Connor on the spot, she realized, but if the man ever intended to be a part of their lives, he needed to get a glimpse of everything.

Raine suddenly looked worried. "He might tell me no."

She gave the top of his wet head an affectionate scruff. "I tell you no sometimes, too. But that doesn't hurt you."

Pursing his lips, he admitted, "It makes me mad when you tell me no."

Laughing, she gave his bottom a playful swat and ushered him out of the room. "You go watch for Connor, while I finish getting dinner ready."

Since Connor's shift had ended earlier today, he'd had plenty of time to change out of his uniform before going to Jazelle's. However, as he'd pulled on his jeans and a button-up shirt, Raine and his fascination for Connor's badge, had crossed his mind.

Now, as he parked his truck behind Jazelle's old vehicle, he wondered if the boy would be pleased with the little gift he'd brought him.

"Connor! You're here!"

Connor barely had time to climb to the ground before Raine was at his side, grinning up at him. His little freckled face was just as dear as he remembered and Connor was amazed at how happy it made him to see the child again.

"Well, look at you! I think you've grown an inch since I've seen you!"

He let out a loud giggle. "Mommy says she's going to put a rock on my head if I keep growing taller."

"Oh, no," Connor said with a chuckle. "We won't let her do that. You're going to be a tall man."

"Like you?"

"Sure. Maybe even taller." He placed a hand on Raine's shoulder and urged him toward the house.

"Wow. Then we'll be alike. That'll be fun!"

The child was assuming Connor would be around by the time he grew to six feet tall and, considering that Raine was five going on six, that meant at least ten years into the future. Connor never planned ahead more than a few days at a time, much less a whole year. He'd never promised anyone he'd be around for the long haul. Except for Joseph. He'd always promised to have his partner's back, to be there if he ever needed him. But Raine was a different matter. Sticking around for the boy's future meant he'd be with Jazelle.

"It's fun to be a kid, too," Connor told him as they stepped onto the porch. "You get to play all the time. I have to work."

"I want to work. I want to be a deputy like you and Uncle Joe," he said and then looked sheepishly up at Connor. "But sometimes I want to be like Uncle

Holt and ride horses. He's a real cowboy. Did you know that?"

Smiling, Connor patted his shoulder. "Yes, I do know that Holt's a real cowboy. Can you ride a horse?"

Raine gave him an emphatic nod. "Don't tell Mommy, but I can hold the reins all by myself. She thinks I'm too little to do that, but Nick says I'm plenty old enough. And Victor is nice. He doesn't act wild."

"Who is Victor?" Connor wanted to know, while thinking if anyone had told him before that he would like having a conversation with a five-year-old, he would've laughed. But damn, if he didn't enjoy listening to every word that came out of the boy's mouth.

"That's Hannah's pony—when she was a little kid like me. Victor is getting old, but Nick says he has plenty of years left. That's good, 'cause I want to keep riding him."

Even though Connor didn't know all the Hollister children personally, he'd heard enough about them from Joseph to know which kids belong to each sibling. Nick was Blake's teenage son and Hannah was Vivian's daughter. From the way Raine talked about everyone on Three Rivers, Connor could tell the boy considered them family. That was a good thing, since Jazelle was the only real family who had a part in the child's life.

Raine opened the door and Connor followed him

into the living room. Presently, the television was on, but the volume was turned too low to pick up the sound of running horses and firing guns of the old Western playing out on the screen. In the direction of the kitchen, he could hear a clank of metal along with the buzzing of a timer.

"Mommy! Mommy! Connor is here!" the boy yelled.

A few seconds passed before Jazelle stepped into the living room, carrying a dish towel and a wide smile on her face.

"Hello," she said. "I see that Raine let you in. Has he already been talking your ear off?"

"Well, we've been having a fine conversation, if I say so myself."

"That's good," she said then gestured toward the couch and chairs grouped in a U shape in the middle of the room. "Have a seat and I'll bring you something to drink."

"Thanks, I'll have a seat, but I'll wait for dinner to have the drink," he told her, giving her a conspiring wink. "I have a little gift for Raine that I want to give him before we eat."

The child's wide eyes flew back and forth between Connor and his mother. "I'm gonna get a gift?"

"Sounds like it," Jazelle said, walking further into the room.

"Let's go over here and sit on the couch," Connor told the boy.

Raine raced over to the couch and flopped onto

the middle cushion, wiggling with anticipation as Connor eased onto the adjacent cushion.

He said, "Okay, Raine, before I give this to you, I want you to promise that you'll take care of it. Is that a deal?"

"Yeah! I'll take real good care of it. Like my arrowhead. See, I keep it down in my pants, like this, all the time." He dug into the front pocket of his jeans and pulled out the piece of flint he'd found at Lake Pleasant.

It was shiny from being handled so much and the fact that Raine considered the arrowhead such an important item touched Connor in a way he didn't understand. Moreover, it scared him to even try to analyze the feelings this child evoked in him.

"That's a safe place to carry it," Connor told him. Then, clearing his throat, he pulled a flat white box from the back pocket of his jeans and placed it on Raine's knees. "This is yours to keep from now on."

Raine promptly jerked off the lid, then stared in openmouthed wonder at the shiny badge nestled on a piece of black felt.

Finally, he blew out a loud breath and squealed with delight. "A badge! Oh, wow! A real badge! Mommy, look!"

Moving closer, she peered down at the gift Connor had given her son. "Yes, I see." She turned a questioning look on him. "It looks like an actual badge."

"It is. I thought…well, that Raine might like having it. And don't get the idea that I'm doing early recruiting," he told her jokingly.

She laughed and the soft light in her eyes was like a kiss on his lips. The connection was like nothing he'd felt before.

"That never entered my mind," she said gently. "I'm thinking that you're a pretty good kind of guy."

Raine continued to stare down at the badge as if he'd been handed the most precious thing on earth. "Can I pick it up and hold it?" he asked.

"Sure. You can even pin it to your shirt. But you should only wear it here at home," Connor told him. "We don't want people getting mixed up and thinking you're a real deputy. Is that okay?"

"Yeah!"

Raine lifted the badge and held it up to his T-shirt. Instead of trying to pin it on himself, he handed it to Connor.

"You put it on me," he said. "So it'll be in the right spot."

Connor was taking in Raine's huge smile when that strange feeling—the one that felt like everything had gone soft and mushy—suddenly returned to his chest. Damn it all, he was going to have to see a doctor, he decided. His heart was giving out on him.

Hell, Connor, you've never had a heart. Not since your father died. Not since you realized that it was meant for you to be all alone in this world.

Shaking away the miserable voice in his head, he

finished the task of pinning on the badge and then ruffled the top of Raine's hair.

"Now you're my honorary deputy sheriff," he told the boy. "What do you think?"

Expecting Raine to let out a loud whoop, or leap up and race around the room, Connor was totally caught off guard when the boy jumped straight into his lap. Without a word, he wrapped his arms tightly around Connor's neck and buried his face against his shoulder.

The fierce hug went on for so long that Connor started to wonder if the boy was fighting back tears. Over the top of Raine's head, he looked helplessly at Jazelle.

She answered softly, "I think he's just a little overwhelmed."

He wasn't by himself, Connor realized. Raine was clinging to him in a way that was causing him to remember years back to when he'd clung to his own father for comfort and love. Losing him, and that solid anchor he'd provided, had torn everything out of Connor. He'd never gotten that part of himself back. Not until this very moment.

Choking back the hot lump of emotion in his throat, Connor gently patted Raine's back. "Everything is okay, Raine. We're buddies now. We'll always be buddies."

Thankfully, his words appeared to do the trick. Raine lifted his head and planted a big kiss on Connor's cheek.

"Yeah, buddies forever!" He climbed down off Connor's lap and began to strut around the room. "I'm honor-ee-ary, Mommy! See?"

Laughing now, Jazelle caught her son by the shoulders and, using her head, motioned for Connor to follow. "Come on, Mr. Honorary Deputy," she said to Raine, "it's time to eat."

For dinner, Jazelle served barbecued short ribs, baked beans and potato salad. For anyone who didn't want ribs, there was also grilled chicken seasoned with garlic and rosemary.

"Blake entertained a few cattle buyers today," Jazelle explained as she passed a basket of yeast rolls to Connor. "And Reeva always cooks a ton of food when cattle or horse buyers come to the ranch. She has this theory that a full stomach opens a man's wallet."

"I don't think the cook need worry about Three Rivers cattle or horses selling. But I'm glad she went overboard," Connor told her. "This is delicious."

"Mommy can cook delicious, too," Raine said. "Grandma Reeva taught her. Didn't she, Mommy?"

Just as Connor was wondering about the child calling Reeva his grandmother, Jazelle said, "Actually, Reeva is Raine's godmother, but he calls her "grandma". And as far as her teaching me how to cook, she's still in the process of teaching me, but I'll never be able to make things taste like hers."

"Mommy makes yummy pancakes," Raine told

Connor, "but she says I can't eat them all the time. She makes me eat oatmeal 'cause it's good for me. Yuk. I bet your mommy never made you eat oatmeal."

Before Connor could decide how to answer that question, Raine shot another one at him.

"Do you have a Mommy?"

"No," Connor admitted. "I'm not as lucky as you, little partner."

Gnawing on a rib, Raine continued to regard him with typical childlike curiosity. "How come you don't have a mommy? Did she die?"

"Raine!" Jazelle scolded. "It's not polite to ask a guest personal questions. Especially with food in your mouth."

Connor frowned at her. "I'd like to think I'm more than a guest. And it's perfectly fine for Raine to ask me anything. He wants to learn."

Her expression rueful, she reached over and clasped her hand around Connor's forearm. "I'm sorry. I didn't mean the word 'guest' literally. And I...well, I don't want Raine to make you uncomfortable. That's all."

"He's not. It's okay," he assured her, then looked across the table at Raine. "My mother didn't die. When I was a tiny baby, she had to go somewhere far away to live."

"Oh." He nodded as though Connor's explanation made perfect sense to him. "That's what Mommy says about my daddy. He had to go far away and we won't ever see him again."

Connor felt sick. Not for himself, but for the pain Jazelle and her son had gone through because of a selfish man.

Like you, Connor? How many women have you used and discarded?

The taunting voice going off in his head angered Connor. He'd never made promises to a woman. He'd never so much as said the word "love" to any of them. The women he'd known had been like him—users. None of them had expected, or even wanted, wedding rings and vows of forever.

But Jazelle was different. She wasn't a user. She was a giver. And he could only wonder how much he could take from her until she started demanding something in return.

"Someday Mommy is gonna find me a real daddy. And he won't ever have to go away. Then I'll be like Little Joe and Nick."

Jazelle didn't comment on her son's prediction, but Connor could feel her gaze sliding over his face. What was she thinking? That he could be the daddy that would never go away?

Oh, Lord, she'd told him there were no hidden strings in her bed. So why did Connor already feel heavy ropes wrapping around him and growing tighter with each passing minute?

"That would be nice, Raine," Connor told him.

Jazelle suddenly cleared her throat and scraped

back her chair. "Well, I don't know about you two, but I'm almost ready for dessert. I'll make coffee to go with it."

"Ignoring his mother, Raine looked at him and asked, "Do you think I'll like coffee when I get big?"

Connor couldn't help but laugh. "Raine, I think when you get big, you're going to like a whole lot of things."

After they finished the meal, the three of them went to the living room where Raine pulled out a set of miniature ranch figures, along with a toy barn and sections of plastic fence.

Connor watched the boy attempt to put the pieces together until he felt compelled to join the child on the floor and help him complete the task. They'd finished making the corrals and were placing the horses inside the barn, when Jazelle sank down next to Connor.

"I want to play, too," she said. "That painted pony is the one I want to ride way over here to gather cattle."

"Do you know how to ride a horse?" Connor asked her.

"I sure do," she told him. "You don't think I've worked on Three Rivers for seven years without learning something about being a cowgirl. But if you really want to see an expert horsewoman, you need to see Maureen or Holt's wife, Isabelle, in action. They're the real deal."

She picked up the brown-and-white plastic horse and pretended to trot it away from the make-believe ranch yard.

Raine hollered, "Whoa, Mommy! That's horse stealin' and since I'm the honor-ee-ary deputy now, I got to arrest you."

Chuckling, Jazelle glanced at Connor. "I think that badge has gone to his head."

Connor grinned. "It happens sometimes."

She turned a pleading look on her son. "Oh, no, Mr. Deputy! Please don't put me in jail. I'll put the horse right back in the barn where he belongs."

"Well, I guess it'll be okay this time," Raine told her. "But next time you want a horse, you have to ask permission first."

"Ah, permission. Now why didn't I think of that?" she asked playfully.

"Because grown-ups don't think they have to ask permission," Raine answered. "They only think kids have to."

Connor laughed out loud. "He's on his way to making a good lawman."

She pulled a face at both of them. "Oh, you two are too smart for your own britches."

The ranch play went on for a few more minutes until Jazelle eventually rose from the floor and announced she was going to go clean the kitchen.

"I'll come help you," Connor offered.

She quickly shook her head. "No. You'll be a big help if you stay here and keep Raine occupied."

"Mommy, can me and Connor watch the dog show?"

"Dog show?" Connor asked curiously.

"Old reruns of the famous collie," Jazelle explained. "Raine loves them."

"*Lassie*?" Connor asked with surprised.

"Yeah! *Lassie*!" Raine exclaimed. "She's really smart. She barks and gets Timmy out of trouble!"

Jazelle glanced at her watch. "Okay. Hurry and get these toys put away and go put on your pajamas. It's almost time for the show to start."

Twenty minutes later, with Raine snuggled close to his side, Connor watched the television screen as the really smart collie spotted the beginning of a forest fire and was racing back home to alert his master.

Surprised that the child wasn't cheering the dog on, Connor glanced down to see Raine had fallen sound asleep right in the middle of the exciting climax.

Thinking Jazelle might show up from her kitchen duty, he decided to watch the last five minutes of the program. But as soon as the credits began to roll, he squared around on the cushion and lifted the sleeping child up and into his arms.

Since he'd been in Raine's bedroom before, he knew where to go. Once he stepped through the door, he used his shoulder to push up the light switch on the wall. It caused a small lamp near the bed to flicker on and he was grateful to see that Jazelle had already turned down the cover on the twin bed.

Once he placed Raine on the mattress and adjusted the pillow beneath his head, he pulled the thin cover up to his waist, then reached to unpin the badge from the pocket of his striped pajamas. Throughout it all, the child never stirred and Connor found himself gazing down at the long lashes resting upon his cheeks, the freckles dusting his nose and the thick blond hair covering one eyebrow.

Right now Jazelle was managing to keep the boy on the right track. But how would it be when he grew into those challenging years? From his own rowdy behavior as a teenager, Connor knew Raine would need the firm hand of a father to guide him into manhood and to make sure he understood the rules of right and wrong.

If not for having a solid friend like Joseph during those years, Connor would've probably wound up in juvenile detention. But thankfully he'd wanted to emulate Joseph's good morals and somehow he'd managed to soak up part of his friend's strong character. Not enough to be a father, though. Oh, no. Raine deserved the best. Not just an imitation.

Breathing deeply, Connor turned away from Raine's bed and placed the badge right next to the arrowhead that was lying on top of the chest of drawers.

Can we go hunt for arrowheads again, Connor? That was fun. Really fun.

Raine had put the question to Connor during dinner and he'd not been able to refuse the child. Rather, he'd promised to take him as soon as he had a free day from work.

Connor's answer to the boy had promptly landed Jazelle's thoughtful gaze on the side of his face. What had she been thinking? That things with the three of them were getting out of hand? Or had she been surprised that Connor had even bothered to consider Raine's wants and wishes?

Not wanting to think any further than tonight, Connor walked over to the doorway and turned off the light. Through the semidarkness of the room, he glanced one last time at the sleeping child, then turned and headed to the kitchen to find Jazelle.

Jazelle was standing at the sink, drying the last of the dishes, when she felt Connor's arms slip around her waist and the front of his body press against the back of hers.

"Mmm. You taste better than the custard pie we had for dessert," he said as he sprinkled kisses against the side of her neck.

Goose bumps erupted along the backs of her arms as Jazelle closed her eyes and savored having him close.

"And I'm not as fattening, either," she said through a wide smile.

Chuckling, he used his nose to nuzzle away the fabric of her blouse so that his lips could move to the ridge of her shoulder.

"It's a good thing or I'd already have twenty extra pounds on me."

She placed the glass on a dish towel spread across the countertop, then turned so that the front of her body crushed up against his and her eyes focused on his rugged face.

"Where's Raine?" she asked. "Asleep in front of the TV?"

"No. He's asleep in bed. Lassie was just about to save the day when I noticed he was out like a light, so I carried him to bed. And put his badge on the chest of drawers with his arrowhead," he told her.

"Thank you. That was a nice thing for you to do," she told him. "So was giving him the badge. How did you manage to have an extra one? I'm assuming they're not something that's often handed out."

Connor shrugged. "You're right, they aren't. But this one happened to have a little flaw on the front of it, so the department ordered me another one."

"Flaw or not, Raine considers it priceless." Her smile provocative, she slipped her arms around his waist and pulled herself tighter to his hard body. "So, are you ready for another round of TV or do you have, uh, something else on your mind?"

For an answer, he lowered his head and Jazelle was quick to lift her mouth to his.

The kiss he placed upon her lips started as a gentle tease but rapidly deepened into a hungry search. At the same time, his hands urgently roamed over her shoulders, across her back, then around to her breasts.

As soon as his fingers began to knead the soft flesh, she groaned and pressed her hips against the hard bulge pushing at the fly of his jeans. These past few days she'd desperately wanted to make love to him again and now that she was actually standing in his arms, the need was totally consuming her.

When he finally lifted his head, he was breathing hard and his features were taut and strained. "I guess showing you what's on my mind will have to wait," he said ruefully.

Her brain was already so fogged with desire, she struggled to follow his words. "Wait?" she asked huskily. "Why? Did you get a call and need to leave?"

Frustration twisted his features. "No. But Raine is in the house."

She looked at him with disbelief and then a low chuckle rumbled out of her. "Of course he's in the house. It's where he's supposed to be."

He grimaced. "Yes, but we, uh, can hardly be together with him here."

She nearly laughed a second time, but her amusement vanished as she suddenly realized this whole thing with her and Raine was a totally new situation for him.

Cradling his face with both hands. "Oh, Connor, what do you think married parents like Joe and Tessa do? Never have sex, or send the kids out to the barn to sleep with the horses?"

He groaned. "No. But Raine might wake up and…"

When his words trailed off, she said, "He always sleeps through the night. And even if something did happen to wake him, we'll make sure the bedroom door is shut."

Doubts continued to flicker across his face. "I'm not sure I feel right about this, Jazelle."

So far tonight, she'd been getting the impression that Connor felt comfortable with idea of the three of them at home in a family setting. He'd even seemed to enjoy the playtime with her son. But somewhere between then and now, something had changed. Or maybe that was the whole problem, she thought. Nothing had actually changed to make him want to be a part of a family.

An uneasy feeling washed through her and she turned away from him to stare blindly at the cabinet counter. "I think I understand," she said dully. "So, if you'd rather…we can go watch TV or play cards. Or, wonder of wonders, we could even talk. You know, that thing we do with our lips when we're not kissing."

He muttered a curse and then his hands were on her shoulders, spinning her around until she was facing him.

"Damn it, you know what I want!"

Resting her palms against the middle of his chest, she looked into his blue, blue eyes. "You can't have everything exactly like you want it, Connor. I have a child. And he's a part of this—of me. If you can't deal with that, then we don't have a chance of making it out of this kitchen together, much less going as far as the bedroom."

His nostrils flared. "That's pretty blunt."

"I'm trying to be real with you, Connor. You need to understand that I'm not the same gullible young woman who allowed a man to lead her around by the heartstrings. For my own sake, and for Raine's, I can't be that soft anymore."

He studied her for a long moment before he bent his head and kissed her with a passion so hot it stole her breath and wobbled her knees.

"I don't want you to be soft," he whispered against her cheek. "I just want you to make love to me."

Jazelle wrapped her hand around his and, as she led him to her bedroom, wondered how much longer he would allow her to hold on to him. How much longer would it be before he felt the urge to move on to a woman who wasn't tied to a young child? How long before he realized he didn't want the love she was so desperately trying to give him?

Chapter Eleven

"Joe, did you always want to marry Tessa?"

Behind the steering wheel of his truck, Joseph took his eyes off the highway long to glance at Connor. "Not exactly. I mean, I had to fall in love with her first. At the time we met, she had a lot going on in her life. Remember, we were trying to figure out why Ray Maddox had willed the Bar X to her?"

"Yes, I remember. I also remember how shocked everyone was when you learned Ray was actually her father," Connor told him. "So when did you realize you wanted her to be your wife?"

It was Wednesday morning and, for the past hour, the two men had been traveling south on Highway 80 to Phoenix. Now the skyline of the city had finally emerged on the distant horizon and, in a matter of minutes, they'd be at the huge Maricopa County livestock sale barns. Behind the seat on the back floorboard of the truck, a stack of flyers waited to be dispensed to anyone willing to take one.

Joseph chuckled. "I guess it was when I figured out I couldn't live a day without her in it. Why are you asking? Have you reached that point with Jazelle?"

He'd reached a point all right, but not the one Joseph was talking about. Three nights ago, when he'd spent part of the night at Jazelle's house, something cataclysmic had happened to him. And when he'd finally climbed out of her bed and driven home, he'd recognized that their time together had to end.

Call him a prude or old-fashioned, but he'd not wanted Raine to find him there the next morning. He wanted the boy to see him as a man to admire and look up to, not one who crept in and out of his mother's bed. And then there was Jazelle. She deserved more than he could give her. She deserved love and commitment. A husband who'd cherish her and make her happy. He wasn't that man. And from the way she'd looked at him when he'd left her house the other morning, he had the sick feeling she was already beginning to see he wasn't the right man for her.

Connor grunted. "Hell, Joe, I don't know what's happening with me. I think… These last few days— I guess I was reminded that if a man wants Jazelle in his life, he has to understand that Raine is a part of the package."

"You knew that before you ever went out with her."

He blew out a heavy breath. "Yeah. I sure did. I just didn't realize that he would…"

When he failed to finish, Joseph directed a frown at him. "What's the matter? Is Raine getting on your nerves?"

No, he was making a mess of his heart, Connor could've told him. The more time he spent with the boy, the more he wanted to think of him as his son. But that was wrong. He couldn't be Raine's father. That meant marriage to Jazelle. That meant making a home for the three of them. What did Connor really know about those things? Sure, he could make them happy for a few hours at a time. But 'round-the-clock, day in, day out was something different.

Life was full of bumps and bruises. Illnesses, job situations and financial strains always seemed to hit at the worst times. He could deal with his own problems, but how could he possibly know the right course to take if those difficulties included Jazelle and Raine? To try would only end up making a mess of his life and theirs.

Clenching his jaw at the painful thought, he glanced at Joseph. "No. He's a precious little boy. I think…well, to be honest, I've gotten too damned attached to him."

Joseph grunted. "If you ask me, I think you're getting a whole heck of a lot attached to Jazelle, too."

Connor didn't bother to argue that fact. Like a fool, he'd allowed his feelings to rule his thinking. He wasn't just attached to Jazelle, he was besotted with her. And that could only mean one thing. He had to find the strength to walk away and never look back.

Ten minutes later, the men arrived at the auction barn. With the sale set to start in less than an hour, vehicles and livestock trailers were already parked in every available space surrounding the facility.

Joseph parked as close as he could manage and the two of them collected a sizable stack of flyers from the back and headed to toward the gathering crowd of buyers and spectators.

"I'm not that familiar with livestock auctions," Connor said as they neared the front of the big barn enclosing the sale ring. "I wasn't expecting this many people to be here."

Off to the side of the huge structure made of corrugated iron, rows and rows of corrals constructed of green pipe contained herds of cattle and horses.

"These things are big deals to farmers and ranchers. Dad mostly came down here because it's a meeting place for friends and acquaintances. And sometimes he'd get lucky and pick up a few nice head of cows or bulls. Mom always used to joke that sale day was Dad's escape from workday. Here, lately,

I've been wondering if sale day might have turned out to be his undoing."

"Do you think Joel might have put his trust into someone that wasn't what he, or she, seemed?" Connor asked. "Maybe one of his transactions involving livestock turned sour."

"I've wondered that same thing over and over." He gave his head a helpless shake. "I can only hope we get some kind of lead today."

By the time they entered the busy barn, the auction had started and the speakers positioned around the building blasted out the rapid-fire words of the auctioneer attempting to entice the crowd to purchase a small herd of Hereford cows. Along with the auctioneer's loud voice, bid spotters shouted, cattle bawled and metal gates clanged as animals were moved from one small pen to the next.

In the middle of the melee, Joseph and Connor put their heads together and eventually decided that one would deal with handing flyers to the general public, while the other approached the men and women working in different capacities around the facility.

Connor volunteered to take on the workers, which turned out to be more difficult than he'd first imagined. Most of them were clearly annoyed to be interrupted for any reason, much less to answer questions about a woman who'd visited the sale some seven years ago. Many of the younger workers Connor approached hadn't even been around at the time and, unfortunately, the older ones drew blanks.

After about an hour and a half of getting nowhere, Connor decided to find Joseph to check on his partner's progress. As he departed the back area of the barn, where the horses were penned, he spotted an older cowboy with a plaster cast on his forearm opening and closing a gate. Since he was the only worker in this section of the building that Connor hadn't questioned, he decided to give the man a try.

After quickly introducing himself, Connor handed him one of the flyers and explained that he was helping a friend search for a woman.

The gray-haired cowboy, who'd introduced himself as Caspar, shoved a black hat off his forehead and squinted at the information on the flyer. "Joel Hollister, huh? I remember him. Hell of a cowboy. Rich as cream on a churn paddle, too. You wouldn't ever know that from talking with him, though. Everybody liked him."

Connor felt a spark of hope. "You knew him?"

"Oh, yeah. Knew him well. He came down here to the sale most every week or every other week. I always told him if I thought there was a good horse he might be interested in. He had a boy, you know, that trained horses. Guess he still does. Now that Joel is gone, I don't hear about the family."

"That would be Holt. Yes, he still trains horses. In a very big way," Connor told him then ventured to ask, "The woman we're trying to find was supposedly seen with Joel here at the sale from time to time.

We don't know who she might've been, but we think she might possibly know something about his death."

Caspar frowned at him. "His death? Thought that was an accident. That's what the paper claimed."

"Well, yes," Connor told him. "But the family doesn't think so."

Tapping a gnarled finger against the flyer, Caspar said, "This woman—was she a relative or something?"

"No. We don't actually know who she was. She might've been buying livestock or she might even have worked here. We just don't know. Do you have any idea?"

"What did she look like?"

"The only thing we know is that she was blond and maybe medium height."

He pinched the bridge of his nose, then slowly began to nod. "There was a blonde who used to work here. Cooked hot dogs and hamburgers and that sort of thing in the concession stand. A few times I saw her and Joel having coffee together."

Connor was so excited he wanted to grab the old cowboy and hug him. "Are you going to be here for a while? I mean right here?" He pointed to the spot where they were standing. "I want you to talk to my friend—he's Joel's youngest son."

"Sure, I'll be here till the lights go out."

Connor hurried out to the seating around the sales ring, thinking Joseph might be there. When he failed to spot him, he pulled out his phone and punched Joseph's number.

As soon as he answered, Connor practically shouted, "Wherever you are, get the heck over here! I'll be waiting for you behind the bleachers at the sale ring."

"Why? What's up?"

"I've found someone who remembers the blonde—and your dad!"

The phone went dead and Connor could only imagine what was going through his friend's mind.

Two minutes later, Joseph was matching his long strides to Connor's as the two men hurried down a back alleyway toward the horse pens.

"What made you come way down here, anyway?" Joseph asked.

"You know me, Joe, leave no stone unturned. And I saw this old man and decided to give him a try."

"Do you know what this might mean to me—to the family?" he asked then said, "No. I can't let my hopes get to out of hand. Not before we talk to the guy."

When they reached the area where Caspar was working, they found the old man busy filling water troughs in a pen several yards away. As soon as he spotted Connor and Joseph, he waved and yelled, "Be there in a minute."

Once he finally made his way over to the two deputies, he immediately stuck his hand out to Joseph.

"I'm Caspar Garza and you must be Joel's son," he said. "You look a bit like him."

"Thanks, Caspar. I'm Joseph Hollister," he said as he heartily pumped the man's hand. "And you can't imagine how happy I am to meet you."

"Well, I don't know how I can help, but I'll try."

"Connor tells me you remember a woman and Dad having coffee together. Do you happen to know her? Or remember her name?"

Caspar thoughtfully rubbed his grizzled chin. "I didn't know much about her. Just passed a few words with her whenever I visited the concession. She would've been pretty if she hadn't been so haggard. You know, like she was always worn down to a frazzle. She was a hard worker."

Connor and Joseph exchanged questionable glances and Caspar continued to rub his chin.

After a moment he said, "I do believe her name was Ginny. That's it. Ginny Patterson."

Connor made a triumphant fist pump while Joseph exhaled a huge breath of relief.

"This Ginny doesn't work here anymore?" Joseph quickly asked.

"No. Quit a long time ago. Come to think of it, after I read about your dad's death, I never seen her around. Didn't put those two things together, though." He squinted curiously at Connor then Joseph. "Is there some connection?"

"We don't know, Mr. Garza," Joseph told him. "She's the only clue we have, and we're hoping she might give us some helpful information. Would you happen to know where she lives?"

"Don't have a clue. But I figure she lived somewhere in Phoenix. That old car she drove smoked like a chimney. It couldn't make it more than a few blocks at a time. Guess her husband couldn't do any better for her."

Both Connor and Joseph shook Caspar's hand and thanked him soundly.

"Good luck to you both," he said. "And if you need me again, I work here every day."

Deciding they'd gained enough information from Caspar, the two men thanked him and left the building. By the time they reached the truck and climbed inside, Joseph was so overcome with emotion, he dropped his forehead on the top of the steering wheel and remained that way for long moments.

"It's going to be okay, Joe," Connor said gently. "You need to be happy."

"I am, Connor. It's just that…it's been so many years with nothing more than tiny pieces of Dad's shirt and a rowel off his spur. Now, all of a sudden, we might actually be getting close to the truth. It feels surreal. It's…a lot to take in at once."

Joseph's voice was choked and Connor realized the man wasn't far from tears. The two of them were brothers by choice, not by happenstance of birth, and Connor could hardly bear to see him hurting for any reason.

Without a word, Connor climbed out of the truck,

went around to the driver's-side door and opened it. "Scoot over," he told him. "I'm driving."

"That isn't necessary."

"I didn't say it was. I just said I'm driving. You get over there in the other seat and see if you can pull up any Ginny Pattersons living here in Phoenix. If we're lucky, we might locate her before the day is out."

A few minutes later, the two men found a fast-food restaurant and, while consuming burgers and fries, were searching through a fairly lengthy list of Pattersons that had popped up during Joseph's search on his smartphone.

"Too bad we can't use the department database," Connor said. "But Jerry's working the system today and he's a stuffed shirt. Now, if Nancy was on duty, she'd run the name for us and text us the list."

"No matter. I've found plenty to start with," Joseph told him. "If need be, we can use the database when we get back to the office."

"Well, the way Caspar talked, this Ginny that worked at the sale barn was financially strapped," Connor reflected. "I figure we'd be wasting time to look at the Pattersons in the ritzy part of the city."

"You're right." Joseph agreed with his reasoning. "Unless the woman married into money since she worked there."

"That's unlikely. What about this one?" He pointed to one of the addresses Joseph had copied onto the page of a tiny notebook.

Joseph scrolled through the city map he'd called up on his phone. "Doesn't look far from here. The next one is fairly close, too." He put down the phone and began gathering up the last of his meal. "If you're finished eating, let's go see what we can find."

Hours later, after talking with Ginny Patterson number five and still no luck, Connor's spirits began to dip. "I'm beginning to wonder if the Ginny Patterson we're looking for has moved away from Phoenix," he said. "If she was involved in your father's murder, she might've fled the area a long time ago."

Joseph heaved out a weary breath. "That's a possible theory. But years have passed since Dad's death. The person or persons involved most likely believe they're in the clear. Especially since the case was ruled an accident. I'm betting the woman is still around."

Since Joseph's intuitions were usually right, Connor could hardly argue. "There's another Ginny a few blocks from here," he said. "We might as well check her out before we call it a day."

Joseph agreed and within five minutes they were driving through a rundown neighborhood of old row houses. Vehicles were parked along the curbs, while trash littered the yards and street.

"This looks real cheerful," Connor said grimly. "Reminds me of the neighborhood where my uncle used to live."

"Most of the house numbers are torn off or too

faded to read," Joseph remarked as he peered out the windshield.

Connor suddenly pointed to a small beige stucco on the right side of the street. "That's it—1121."

Joseph turned onto the short drive and braked the truck to a stop behind an older model white car with a crumpled trunk and an Arizona Cardinal logo plastered to the back windshield. To the left of the driveway, two large mixed-breed dogs were barking fiercely and doing their best to climb the sagging chain-link fence that squared off a small front lawn. Even if his life depended on it, Connor couldn't have found a blade of grass anywhere on the patch of ground.

"Great," Connor said as they climbed out of the truck. "I can already see the two of us sitting in an emergency room waiting to get stitched up."

"The fence will hold the dogs," Joseph told him. "Let's just get this over with."

At the front door, Joseph knocked while Connor stood and scanned the area around them. Even in the capacity of a deputy sheriff, he wouldn't want to be in this neighborhood after dark. Actually, he didn't deem it safe even in the light of day.

"This isn't exactly a place I'd like to go Christmas caroling," Connor muttered under his breath.

Joseph was about to reply when the door suddenly creaked partially open and a woman's face emerged around the edge. She looked to be somewhere in her sixties with blond hair that came from a bottle and gray eyes that mirrored years of struggles.

"Are you two lost?" she asked, her gaze encompassing both Joseph and Connor. "You don't look like you belong around here."

"No, ma'am," Joseph told her. "We're from Yavapai County. We're looking for a woman. A Ginny Patterson."

Suspicion suddenly narrowed the woman's eyes. "What do you want with her?"

While the dogs continued to have a snarling, snapping fit in the yard, Connor decided to speak up. "We think she might be able to give us some information we need. Did you ever work at the Maricopa County sale barn?"

"That was a long time ago," she said. "And who are you two, anyway? A pair of cops?"

Connor could see the word *Bingo!* go off in Joseph's eyes.

"No, ma'am." Joseph pulled a personal card from his shirt pocket and handed it to the woman. "We're off-duty deputy sheriffs. I'm Joseph Hollister and he's Connor Murphy. We're trying to gather information on my father's death."

Only a portion of the woman's face was exposed to their view, but it was enough for Connor to see her skin turn a sickly pallid color.

"I don't know nothin' about Joel Hollister's death! And if you two don't get out of here, I'm gonna call some real cops on you!"

Before Joseph could make any sort of reply, she slammed the door, ending any chance to continue the conversation.

"'Real cops,'" Connor said sarcastically. "What the hell are we? Cartoon characters?"

Joseph grimaced. "We're out of our jurisdiction. Plus, we're working on a case that's been closed for years. We're not exactly in a position to make demands."

Connor mouthed another curse word under his breath, then said, "Looks like that's all she wants to say. But she knows plenty."

"Yeah," Joseph muttered then shrugged. "Well, at least we found her. Now if we can just figure out a way to get her to talk."

"Well, I don't know what went wrong," Connor said wryly. "Usually women take one look at you and start spilling their guts."

"Ha! That's the other way around, buddy. They take a look at you and it's like they've had a shot of truth serum. All sorts of information starts spewing out of their mouths."

"It didn't work on this one," Connor said, not bothering to hide his disappointment.

Joseph nudged Connor's shoulder toward the steps leading off the porch. "Come on. Let's get out of here before those dogs break out."

"I thought you said the fence would hold them," Connor reminded him as they quickly strode back to the truck.

"That was before I noticed the gate hanging by one flimsy wire," Joseph told him, gesturing to a metal gate near the end of the porch.

Seeing it, Connor made a grim promise, "The next time we come here, we're going to be wearing our weapons and our badges."

Joseph let out a short, cynical laugh. "What's that going to do? You think a show of force is going to make her talk, or frighten the dogs into silence?"

"No. But it'll make us feel a heck of a lot safer."

By the time Connor got home that night, he'd come to the decision that the fairy tale he'd been living in the past few weeks with Jazelle and Raine needed to come to an end. Putting it off any longer would only make the break worse.

Marriage or nothing. Marriage or nothing. In spite of the eventful day he'd spent with Joseph, the two choices had lingered in the back of his mind. Like a scale with rocks on one side and gold on the other, the options had dipped up and down, one way and then the other, until he was sick of weighing anything regarding his future.

Damn it, he wasn't a hypocrite, but that's what he'd become. He was a fraud, as well as a fool for thinking he could fake his way through a meaningful relationship with Jazelle.

After pacing restlessly through the quiet house, he sat on the couch and punched in her number.

She answered on the second ring and he could

tell from the sound of her voice that she hadn't been expecting him to call at such a late hour.

"I hope you haven't gone to bed yet," he told her. "I would've called sooner, but Joe and I didn't get back from Phoenix until a short while ago."

"It's okay. I'm not yet ready for bed," she told him then asked, "How did things go down there? Any luck?"

He quickly explained what they'd discovered about Ginny Patterson and how she'd refused to talk with them.

"But that hardly means we've given up," he told her. "We've crossed the biggest hurdle by just finding out who the woman is and where she lives. We'll figure out the rest."

"Maureen and the whole family will be overjoyed with this news," she said. "I just hope when it's all said and done, she'll find some peace. She clearly loves Gil, but she won't consider marriage until this thing about Joel's death is settled."

Love and marriage. Damn it, why did it feel like every conversation, every thought he possessed, always come back to those two words?

He said, "Uh, well, hopefully the truth will come out soon."

"Yes," she agreed.

He closed his eyes and wearily pinched the bridge of his nose. "The reason I'm calling is... I—I'm wondering if I could see you tomorrow night. I understand it might be a hassle for you, but it would be better if Raine wasn't there."

Silence stretched for so long he thought the cell signal had dropped the call. "Jazelle? Are you there?"

She finally replied, "I thought we worked that out the other night, Connor."

He dragged a hand over his face as memories of that night assaulted him. Yes, he'd gone to bed with her. But all the while, he'd felt as though the walls of her bedroom had been closing in on him. All the while, he'd felt like a lying bastard. Not only lying to her, but lying to himself, also.

Swallowing hard, he said, "I need to talk to you—about some things."

He was met with another pause before she said, "Okay. I might have to ask my mother to watch Raine for me. He'll have a fit about going to see her, but it can't be helped. Not if you don't want him here."

Connor bit back a sigh of frustration. She'd taken his request to talk with her alone and twisted it into a slight against Raine.

"None of this is about Raine. All I want is for the two of us to talk without interruptions. That's all."

If there was a sharpness to his voice, he couldn't help it. All he wanted to do now was to put this painful ordeal behind him.

"All right. I'll see you tomorrow evening," she told him and then hung up before he could say goodbye.

The next morning at Three Rivers Ranch, talk around the breakfast table was all about Joseph and

Connor's heroic efforts of tracking down the mystery woman. Everyone appeared hopeful, especially Gil. He was beaming from ear to ear.

Hardly a surprising reaction from the man, Jazelle thought as she carried an empty carafe of coffee into the kitchen. The retired detective was madly in love with Maureen and wanted to make her his wife.

Someday a man will look at you the way Gil looks at Maureen. Someday you'll be a wife who's loved and cherished by her husband. But not now. Not by Connor.

Entering the kitchen, Jazelle did her best to push the voice of doom out of her head as she quickly crossed the room and went to work starting a fresh pot of coffee.

"The kids have scarfed up all the tortillas and are hollering for more," she said to Reeva. "And Maureen asked for grapefruit."

"I've already heated another batch of tortillas. And there's a second bowl of eggs ready to go. You might as well take those to the table with the tortillas." Reeva left her spot at the stove and walked over to the refrigerator. "I swear sometimes I think I'm cooking for a hotel."

"What are you talking about, Reeva? Cooking for a hotel would be a snap compared to this."

Reeva chuckled as she cut a grapefruit in two and arranged both pieces on a breakfast plate. "That's okay," she said with one of her rare grins. "It's nice to see everyone happy and celebrating this morning. Joe and Connor should be proud of themselves. They'll get to the truth. I feel it in my bones."

Get to the truth. Connor's call last night had managed to jerk Jazelle out of the fairy-tale world she'd been living in for the past month. She'd spent the better part of the night thinking about their relationship and where it might be headed.

When he'd given Raine the badge, she'd been hopeful. The gesture had made her believe he honestly cared about Raine, that he was growing comfortable with being part of a family unit. But then later, when they'd made love, she felt as if he'd been on automatic pilot. His body had gone through the motions, but his thoughts and feelings had been far away. Since that night, she'd not seen him and the few text messages he'd sent her had been brief and stilted.

Jazelle didn't need a picture painted to explain his behavior. He wanted to end things between them. He wanted to move on to some other woman with a less complicated life. Well, she'd known from the very beginning that her time with Connor would most likely be short.

Realizing she had yet to reply to Reeva's comment, she said, "Yes, it's good to see everyone happy and hopeful."

"Everyone except you, Jazelle. You look like you've bit into a green persimmon," Reeva commented as she placed the plate of grapefruit and the bowl of eggs onto a tray. "What's wrong? Are you coming down with something?"

Seeing the coffee was finished dripping, Jazelle poured the fresh brew into an insulated carafe. "I'm not sick. I'm just thinking."

"Bills to pay?"

Bitter reality practically choked her, but somehow she managed to answer. "Yes. A very costly one."

That evening, Jazelle waited as long as she could before driving Raine over to her mother's house, which was located in a quiet residential area of Wickenburg. The dread she felt every time she made a point of seeing her mother always filled Jazelle with guilt. On the other hand, Della had never done much to make her and Raine feel welcomed or wanted, much less loved.

"Mommy, I don't want to go to Grandma Della's. She'll be mean," Raine complained as Jazelle steered her truck into her mother's driveway. "Why can't I stay with you?"

Because Connor had turned out to be no better than Spence, Jazelle thought dismally. He didn't want Raine around whenever he gave her the ax. The idea caused tears to sting the backs of her eyes, but she did her best to blink them away.

"Because I have some important things to do and it will be better for you to be here with Grandma Della while I do them. It won't be for long. I promise." She had no idea if Connor intended his talk with her to be brief or lengthy. Either way, it didn't matter. After an hour, she would pick up Raine and take him home.

Bending his head, the boy mumbled, "Well, I guess it'll be okay."

"Sure it'll be okay. And when I get finished, we might even go out to the Broken Spur and get ice cream. How would that be?"

His head jerked up and he stared at her hopefully. "Really? Can we?"

Jazelle reached over and gave his ear an affectionate tweak. "I promise."

Della Hutton was a tall, buxom woman with dirty-blond hair and sharp brown eyes. At forty-seven, she was still a young woman, but it hardly showed in her appearance or her attitude—which probably accounted for the reason the woman was still single after all these years.

"I wondered how much time was going to pass before you finally showed up," she said as she stepped aside to allow her daughter and grandson into the house.

Biting back a sigh, Jazelle leaned over and pecked an obligatory kiss on Della's cheek. "I've been meaning to stop by for a visit," she said truthfully. "but things have been extra busy out at the ranch."

"The ranch. Oh, yes, that important job you have of waiting on the Hollisters hand and foot," Della said with weary sarcasm. "When are you going to quit being a maid to ranch royalty and get a real job, Jazelle?"

Ignoring her mother's usual put-downs, Jazelle guided Raine over to a long beige couch. As usual, Della kept the house perfectly spotless and the air-conditioning to a chilly setting.

"I like my job just fine, Mom."

"No ambition. That's your problem," she said. "You have too much of your dad in you to ever really excel."

"Everyone has their own definition of excelling, Mom. Mine just happens to be different than yours."

She sniffed. "Well, at least I'm not a waitress."

Her mother had worked for years at the same locally owned insurance company in town. She made a decent salary for answering the phone and taking payments, but it didn't match the one the Hollisters paid Jazelle.

"Like me, you mean?" Jazelle asked pointedly.

Della must've decided she was wasting her time on the subject of jobs, so she suddenly directed the conversation to a different topic. "I don't suppose you've heard from your father lately?"

The prickly matter caused Jazelle's already tight nerves to nearly snap. "No. I'm sure Dad has been busy."

Della snorted as she took a seat in an armchair. "We don't have to guess about that. He's busy working his rear off to raise those two kids of his. He gives them and that wife everything they want. But he wanted the extra load, so I don't pity him."

Della Hutton didn't pity anyone, Jazelle thought sadly. Her heart just wasn't capable of expressing compassion. But it was certainly capable of demonstrating jealousy and greed. Over the years, Jazelle had often prayed that something or someone would come along to change her mother's bitter outlook on life. So far it hadn't happened. Still, Jazelle wasn't going to give up completely. Miracles did happen.

Jazelle glanced pointedly at her watch while trying not to let Raine's dejected expression get to her. So far the little guy hadn't said a word or attempted to approach his grandmother with a hug or kiss. That was because he'd learned Della didn't welcome such displays of affection.

"I have to go, Mom. I'll be back in about an hour to pick up Raine. He's already eaten, so you don't have to bother feeding him."

Della looked over at her grandson, who was sitting stiffly on the edge of the cushion, clutching a backpack to his chest. "As long as he behaves, everything will be fine. But he needs to know right off that he can't go outside. I just had the yard seeded and I don't want it disturbed."

Trying to hang on to her patience, Jazelle said, "Raine has brought a coloring book and crayons with him. He'll entertain himself."

She walked over to Raine and, after giving him a hug and a kiss, hurried to the front door. But before she managed to make an escape, her mother called out, "What's so important this evening that you needed me to watch Raine?"

"I have a meeting with someone, Mom."

Della frowned with disapproval. "A man, no doubt. Jazelle, didn't Spence teach you anything? Men are nothing but users."

It would be easy for Jazelle to fall into the same bitter pit her mother existed in, but she refused to live such a miserable life. For one thing, the Hollister men had showed her that there were genuine, loving men in the world. Whether Jazelle was ever lucky enough to find one was another matter.

"I'll be back for Raine in an hour," she said dully, fleeing through the door before her mother could throw any more sage advice at her.

Chapter Twelve

When Connor arrived at Jazelle's, her truck was gone, so he parked to the side and settled back in the seat to wait for her return. Behind the dark lens of his aviator glasses, he studied the modest house and allowed his mind to go back to the night he and Joseph had responded to the Wallace break-in.

Connor had been flat-out exhausted that night and he'd been annoyed as hell at Joseph for wanting to make a security check on Jazelle's house. Now he could only think of how much the unplanned stop had changed his life.

Meeting Jazelle that night had blown Connor away. Not just because she'd had a pretty face and shapely figure. No. There had been an undefinable something about her that had touched him in a way he'd not understood. Why she was the first and only woman to ever get grip on his heart, he didn't know. Now he was faced with the long, arduous job of untangling his feelings and putting them back where they belonged.

The sound of a vehicle interrupted his troubled thoughts and he glanced around to see Jazelle parking alongside him.

Taking in a deep, bracing breath, he climbed out to meet her.

"You could've gone on into the house," she told him as they met in front of the parked trucks. "I left it unlocked just in case you got here before I made it back home."

He slipped off his sunglasses and dropped them into the pocket of his shirt, while telling his eyes not to take in the pretty sight she made standing there in the sinking sunlight.

"No problem," he said. "I just got here anyway."

Without so much as a smile of greeting, she started toward the porch, leaving him to follow. Clearly, she was still irked over his blunt call last night. Well, that hardly mattered now, he thought grimly.

"Have you eaten?" she asked as the two of them entered the living room. "Raine and I had a quick meal before I took him over to Mom's. But I do have leftovers if you're hungry."

"No thanks." The house seemed unnaturally quiet and he realized it was because Raine wasn't there playing with his toys and chattering about all he'd done at the ranch. "Joe and I had a late lunch at the office."

"Oh, you had to work today?"

"For a few hours. A couple of other deputies needed off to do some personal things, so we filled in."

"I see."

She was wearing the same dress she'd had on the night of the dinner party at Three Rivers. She'd looked enchanting that night and this evening was no different. But it was hardly the dress or the elegant way her hair was pinned back from her face that made him want to jerk her into his arms and kiss her senseless. No. It was the love he knew he would taste upon her lips, the longing he would feel in her arms. He wanted that more than anything.

No woman before Jazelle had even pretended to have genuine feelings for him. Now that he'd had a taste of what real caring felt like, he didn't think he could ever go back to one-night stands, to women who only cared about self-gratification. So that left his future looking pretty damned empty.

She said, "Congratulations are in order, it seems. Everyone at Three Rivers is awfully excited about you and Joe finding the mystery woman."

He shrugged. For Connor, being a deputy had never been about seeking praise or pats on the back. "To be honest, we got lucky."

"No matter if it was luck. You've made progress and everybody is happy."

Happy. He'd thought he'd been a happy man before Jazelle. But that was before he'd learned how it felt to be truly wanted. Now he wondered if happiness was something he wasn't supposed to have in his life.

Giving himself a hard, mental shake, Connor walked over and sank onto the middle of the couch. Jazelle followed and eased down onto the cushion next to him.

He was trying to decide how to start when she said, "After you called last night, Connor, I've done a lot of thinking—about you and me. That is what you wanted to talk about, isn't it?"

He nodded, while wishing he could tear his eyes away from her lips. Just watching them filled him with the desire to kiss her.

"Yeah. We've, uh, been getting pretty close these past couple of weeks," he said then almost laughed at how ridiculous that sounded. They'd been as close as two people could get and then some.

She cleared her throat. "That's exactly what I've been thinking about. We never set out for that to happen."

Connor's gaze dropped to her lap, where her hands were tightly linked together. The grip she had on herself was such that her knuckles were white. Was she wishing she had her fingers around his throat? He wouldn't blame her. It was his fault that any of this had started between them in the first place.

"No. We were just going to enjoy being together. That's all." He hated the huskiness of his voice. It made him sound weak. It made him sound like he still wanted her deep down, where it counted. And he didn't. He couldn't.

"I understand that's how you've always felt about it, Connor. And, to be honest, after you left the other night, I realized Raine's and my life isn't the sort of life you want for yourself. And having an affair with a man isn't the sort of thing I want for myself, or for him." She paused and drew in a deep breath. "That's what I've been thinking and I... I've reached the decision that we shouldn't see each other anymore."

Connor shouldn't have been stunned. After all, he'd orchestrated this meeting as a way to end things with her. But he was staggered that she'd turned the tables on him. In fact, he felt like someone had knocked him flat on his back and every ounce of oxygen in his lungs had left his body.

"You want us to stop seeing each other?"

Lifting her chin, she glanced to a spot across the room. "Wanting and needing are two different things, Connor. And I don't need to mess my life up a second time."

She looked at him and he cringed as he spotted the mist in her brown eyes. This wasn't the way he'd expected this evening to go. He'd not planned on her doing the dumping. And he'd definitely not planned on the excruciating pain that was burning a hole in the middle of his chest.

"You think being with me is a—mistake?"

"Think about it, Connor. If by some twist of fate I became pregnant with your child, you'd be furious. You don't want children. You don't want a wife. I'd end up in the same situation I went through with Spence."

She might as well have whammed him in the face with her fist. "You honestly believe I'd be like him? That I could turn my back on my own child? I thought you knew me better than that, Jazelle. And if that's what you really think, why in hell did you invite me into your bed?"

Hot color swept over her face. "You're leaping to conclusions, Connor! I didn't say you'd turn your back on your child. I said you'd be furious with me. Now come on and be honest about this. You told me more than once that children aren't in your plans. Dear God, you didn't even want to ask me for a date because I had Raine! As to why I invited you into my bed... I'm beginning to wonder if I'd momentarily slipped a cog or two."

The underlying fury in her voice said more to him than her actual words.

Connor was struggling to hang on to his temper and it wasn't just because she was pushing his buttons. No, he was angry at himself. For being a fool. For allowing himself to fall head-over-heels for this woman.

"Okay," he said flatly, "you're right in the fact about me having children. I'm not equipped for the job."

Her gaze landed pointedly on his crotch. "If you ask me, you're perfectly equipped for the job. You just don't want to deal with what comes afterward."

Clenching his jaw, he rose, but as he walked across the room, he realized there was no place for him to go. Not yet. Not before he explained what he was doing there.

Explain what, Connor? You don't have to say another word except "Thank you, Jazelle. Thank you for understanding that I need out of this, that you've made it easy for me to turn tail and run."

The damning voice in his head had him growling like a wary dog. He wasn't running, he told himself. He was trying to do what was best for everyone. So why did he feel like Jazelle was tearing his insides out? Why did he feel as low as the dirt on the bottom of his boots?

Swallowing at the painful lump in his throat, he walked back over to the couch and sank down next to her.

"I'm sorry, Jazelle. You have a right to be angry with me. I'm actually angry with myself. And I don't want us to part like that. The time I've spent with you and Raine has been more special to me than you could ever imagine. But you're right. I don't want to deal with what comes afterward. Not the love, the wedding rings, the babies. No. I'm Connor Murphy, the good-time guy." He looked at her pale, taut face and wondered how he was going to live without seeing her, touching her, loving her. "Just tell me something, Jazelle. When did you decide we needed to end things?"

Her head bent and she was pressing her fingertips to her closed eyelids. "The other night—when you told me you didn't want us to go to bed together with Raine in the house. I realized then that being in a family situation was making you uncomfortable. Being with *me* as a part of that family was making you uncomfortable. At first, I didn't want to accept the truth. I wanted to ignore it."

Connor could've told her that he'd been trying to ignore a lot of things since he'd met her. The instant attraction he'd had for her. Breaking his iron-clad rule of never dating a single mother. And last, but hardly least, he'd been trying like hell to ignore the strange, unexplainable feeling he got in his chest just from being near her.

"I've been doing plenty of ignoring, too," he murmured.

She lifted her head and this time her eyes were more than misty. Tears were on the verge of brimming over the lids and rolling onto her cheeks. "You see, I like you very much, Connor. I more than like you. I really care about you. That's why— Well, when a person cares about someone, he or she doesn't want to make that person miserable by trying to hang on, or trying to change them into something other than what they are. Don't you agree?"

He reached for her hands and his stomach clenched with pain as he wrapped his fingers tightly around hers. "I do agree. And it's good that we both can see that our goals and our future plans are different. But there is the matter of Raine. I told him that we'd always be buddies and I truly meant that. In spite of you and me being…over, I hope that you'll let me see him from time to time."

The tears had slipped and as Connor watched them spill over the edge of her top lip, he hated himself for causing her one moment of pain. Despised himself for not having the courage to try to be the man she needed.

"Of course I don't mind," she murmured thickly. "My only concern is that he's going to ask why you're not coming around—I mean on a regular basis. I'll have to explain things in a way he'll understand. I don't know how I'll go about it, but I'll manage."

"Don't try," he told her. "I'll, uh, come by and see Raine. I'll explain that…well, I'll tell him something."

"Fine," she said bluntly. Then, extricating her hands from his, she stood. "Now I need to go fetch Raine from his grandmother's. I promised him I'd be back in an hour."

Connor stood and wondered why he felt like he'd just ran a marathon in triple-digit heat. "All right," he said. "So I guess this is goodbye."

"Guess so," she said with a solemn nod. "And if you do happen to visit Three Rivers again, don't feel awkward about me being there. As far as I'm concerned, we're still friends."

This is crazy, Connor thought. The two of them had been as close as two people could get. Now they sounded like programmed robots. If this was what love did to a person, then he was damned well glad he was getting out.

"Friends. Sure, why not?"

Leaning forward, he pressed a light kiss on her cheek then turned and walked out of the house before she could see the pain in his eyes.

The following week was extra busy at Three Rivers. With September's arrival, Taggart and the hands were gearing up to move several herds from the Prescott ranges down to the more weather-friendly pastures of Three Rivers.

During this time, extra day hands were hired to help with the massive endeavor, which meant the bunkhouse kitchen needed even more food than usual. Jazelle never cooked or cleaned for the bunkhouse. The cowboys took care of those chores. It was her job to make sure they had all the supplies that were needed. Yesterday she'd spent most of the day in town, gathering up a truckload of groceries, which had meant she'd had to put off doing some of her household chores until today.

Jazelle had thought the added work would help to

distract her thoughts away from Connor. But even with all the cleaning, serving meals, shopping and tending to children, she'd not been able to get the man from her mind or her heart. How did everything around her keep going at its normal pace while her whole existence had seemed to stop?

Jazelle, you were right to end things with Connor. Just like your mother has always been right about men. They're users. And that includes Connor Murphy. He was never going to love you. Not really love you. So why grieve over something you never had?

Because, she answered the taunting voice in her head, deep down she'd held out hope that Connor would come to realize he wanted her and Raine in his life on a permanent basis. That eventually he'd come to recognize he had the makings of a good husband and father.

Everything but the "want to," she thought sadly as she peeled a soiled sheet from Billy's crib mattress.

"Oh, there you are, Jazelle. I've been searching all over for you," Maureen said as she stepped into the nursery that joined Roslyn and Chandler's suite of rooms.

Wadding up the sheet, Jazelle stuffed it under one arm and turned to face the woman. It wasn't often that Maureen quit her outside ranch work before dusk. Seeing her in the house in the middle of the afternoon meant she was planning something out of the ordinary.

"Were you needing me for something, Maureen?"

"I've been trying to find my avocado-green skirt. The one that flares out at the hemline. I can't find it anywhere and I wanted to wear it tonight. Gil is taking me up to Gold Cliffs tonight." She let out a little breathless laugh. "I guess you can tell I'm looking forward to going. It's been so long since I've done anything just for fun that I almost feel like a kid planning to play hooky."

Gold Cliffs was a luxurious casino located in the beautiful forested mountains near Prescott. The establishment offered fine dining and live entertainment, and though Jazelle had often wanted to visit the place, she'd never been able to afford the trip.

"If anyone deserves to play hooky, it's you, Maureen. You work harder than anyone around here," she told her. "The green skirt you've been hunting is at the cleaner's. Remember, there was a little stain on the front."

"Darn, I do remember now. I dropped a piece of buttered bread onto my lap. Oh, well," she said, hardly allowing the missing garment to dampen her high spirits. "I'll find something else to wear. I was considering that blue-leather skirt Vivian gave me for Christmas. The straight one that zips all the way down the side. Do you think it would look...well, over the top?"

Mustering up the best smile she could, Jazelle said, "No. It would be perfect. Just don't let Gil go near the blackjack table. With his eyes on you, he'll never be able to concentrate on the cards."

Maureen laughed and gave Jazelle's shoulders a one-armed hug. "Jazelle, honey, you're good for my ego. And did Reeva tell you that I want you both to take off early tonight? No cooking dinner or cleaning up the mess. Gil and I will be gone, so will Roslyn and Chandler and the kids. Kat will fend for Blake and their bunch."

Go home early? Normally she would appreciate the extra time to catch up on chores at home. But the empty house gave her mind free rein and it always trotted right back to Connor and how much she missed him. At least here at the ranch people were coming and going, kids were playing, and work never ended.

"But, Maureen, there's still plenty more things I could be doing. The pantry needs to be cleaned and I've been planning to polish the floor in the den. It's starting to look dull. Might be a good time to do it with most everyone gone. Especially with you and Holt planning to entertain those horse breeders from California next week."

Maureen suddenly stepped back and swept an observant gaze over Jazelle's face. "If you ask me, you're the one who's looking dull around here. I've asked Reeva if you were sick and she insisted you weren't. But I'm not convinced. These past few days, I've noticed there's something off with you. What's happened? Trouble with your mother?"

Jazelle blew out a long breath. Thankfully, Della knew nothing about her daughter's short-lived affair with Connor. Otherwise she'd never quit lecturing Jazelle about foolishly trusting the wrong man, which, in Della's case, meant any man that was breathing.

"Nothing is going on with Mom," she told Maureen. "She's been her usual self."

"Okay, so you have a different problem." Her eyes narrowed like a shrewd mother who knew when her child was being evasive. "How are things going with you and Connor?"

Jazelle gasped. "How did you know about him and me?"

Maureen laughed lightly. "Honey, you know nothing around here stays a secret."

"Well, I wasn't exactly trying to keep it a secret," Jazelle mumbled. "But no matter. It's already done and over between us."

Maureen's lips pressed together. "So that's why you have such a sad look on your face. Your heart is breaking."

Feeling like a silly fool, Jazelle walked over to a window and stared down at a portion of yard behind the ranch house. "I hate to admit it, Maureen, but I've never felt this awful. Not even when Spence deserted me while I was pregnant. I guess that was because I didn't really love him. But now…"

"You really love Connor."

She sighed. "I didn't intend to. It just happened."

Maureen said gently, "That's the way real love is. It can't be forced or contrived. It just happens."

"You sound like you know."

Maureen walked over and sat in one of the wooden rockers that flanked a small table.

"I should. I loved Joel with all my heart and bore him six children. I didn't plan to fall in love with him. It was just there in my heart before I realized what was happening. And now that Gil is here at Three Rivers…well, I'm feeling like I'm falling all over again."

Jazelle sank into the spare rocker.

"That's good, Maureen. You deserve to be happy and loved. And Gil adores you." Tears sprung to her eyes before she could stop them. "I wish it was that way for me and Connor. But he doesn't want a wife or children. He's been footloose for all these years and wants to stay that way. I knew it and he knew it, so I told him we needed to call it quits before one or both of us got hurt."

"Hmm. What did he say to that?"

"He agreed. To tell you the truth, I think he was getting ready to tell me the same thing. I just beat him to the punch."

Her expression rueful, Maureen shook her head. "Connor grew up hard, with no mother, and his father—Monroe—died at a time his young son needed him the most. All Connor has ever known is scrapping for himself. He's never learned how to include anyone in his life. The only person who comes close to being family to him is my Joe."

Jazelle's heart felt so weak and broken she marveled that it continued to beat. "Yes, he told me about the troubled woman who'd given birth to him. And about his dad dying. We, uh, had that in common, you know. Our parents split up—our home life far from idyllic. All that drew us together, I think." Tears leaked from her eyes and she dashed them away with the back of her hand. "But I believe I was right in ending things."

"Well, I certainly don't!" Maureen muttered emphatically.

Jazelle stared at her. "Why? I don't want to make another painful mistake."

"Looks to me like you've already made a mistake. Seems to me your heart is already broken." She looked over at Jazelle. "You need to remember that all this family stuff is new for Connor. He needs time to adjust to it. Time to get used to the idea of being a husband and father. Maybe you ought to go to him and tell him that you're willing to give him whatever time he needs. Because you love him."

Love. Jazelle hadn't spoken that word to Connor. Not even once. Mostly because she'd felt quite certain he hadn't wanted to hear it. Telling him that she loved him would've been the same as circling him with a barbed-wire fence. He would've been desperate to break free. Even if it meant wounding himself in the process.

"Connor doesn't want to hear that kind of thing, Maureen. Not from me."

"But you wish he did," Maureen said shrewdly.

"Because you love him very much. I can see that, even if you can't."

More tears spilled from Jazelle eyes. "I feel like an idiot, Maureen. After the ordeal I went through with Spence, I was determined to never look at another man. Not because I was bitter like my mother, but because I was afraid of being hurt all over again. Then I met Connor and I didn't want to be scared anymore. Now I'm in love with a man who doesn't love me back. But that's only a part of my misery. I feel awful for Raine. He adores Connor."

Maureen's expression turned regretful. "Have you told Raine anything about this split?"

"Not yet. Connor promised to speak to him about it. But we've not seen or heard from him. Actually, I hope Connor doesn't show. Raine's birthday is coming up and I don't want that time for my son to be ruined. You've probably already heard that Katherine and Roslyn are insisting on giving him a party."

"Reeva let me in on the party plans. And if my daughters-in-law hadn't volunteered to do a party for Raine I would have. Birthday cake is my favorite desert," she added jokingly. "Especially when it's not my birthday."

Rising to her feet, Maureen reached down and tugged Jazelle from the rocker. "Come with me. I want you to help me pick out a blouse to go with the blue leather skirt. You always have good taste."

As Maureen led her down the second-floor landing to her bedroom, Raine sniffed back her tears and tried to smile. "I was already thinking you should wear that navy blouse with the ruffle at the neckline."

Maureen laughed. "Jazelle! I rarely wear that blouse. It shows a bit of cleavage!"

"I know." Jazelle attempted to tease. "That's why I say keep Gil away from the blackjack tables."

Laughing, Maureen paused long enough to give Jazelle a tight hug. "Oh, honey, I just want you to be happy. You will think about what I said about talking with Connor?"

"Yes. I'll think about it," she promised.

But whether she'd ever find the courage to actually confess her love to Connor was a whole other matter.

Chapter Thirteen

The following morning, daylight was still a couple of hours away when Connor and Joseph responded to a call involving two men in a fistfight on the side of the highway outside of Yarnell. Since the deputies had already been patrolling that desolate section of the county, it took them less than five minutes to reach the scene but more than an hour and a half to deal with the aftermath of the drunken brawl.

By the time both injured men were hauled off in an ambulance, their vehicles towed away, and statements taken from a pair of witnesses who'd happened to drive upon the incident, the morning sun was trying to peep over the bare mountains.

"Let's stop at Marie's and get some tacos," Joseph

suggested as he steered the truck toward the little town of Yarnell. "We've not eaten since midnight."

Connor didn't hear Joseph or the intermittent voices of the dispatcher and a deputy going back and forth on the radio. He was already lost in thought as he stared out the window at the passing landscape.

"Connor! Wake up over there!"

A blank frown on his face, he looked over at Joseph. "Did you say something?"

"Hell yes! And in case you're interested, I'm going to stop at Marie's for tacos. If you don't want any, you can watch me eat."

Connor scowled at him. "What are you all riled up about?"

"I'm not riled. I just prefer to have a partner that's actually with me—not off somewhere on a different planet."

Dust billowed as Joseph steered the truck off the highway and braked to a stop in front of a little adobe building with a flat roof and a faded turquoise door flanked by two small windows.

Owned and operated by Marie herself, the woman made the best tacos in the whole county and beyond. Normally, Connor would've run a mile for one of the greasy delicacies, but these past few days, his appetite had done a vanishing act.

Blowing out a heavy breath, Connor dug his wallet out of the back pocket of his jeans and pulled out several bills.

"Here!" he said flatly, tossing the money onto

the console between them. "Get the damned tacos and let's go."

Joseph started to say something then apparently changed his mind. Ignoring the money, he climbed out of the truck.

Once his partner had entered the old adobe, Connor wiped a hand over his face and wondered how much longer he could exist with this heavy emptiness weighing down every thought in his head, every cell in his body. He'd known that ending things with Jazelle would be hard, but he hadn't counted on the crushing pain that plagued him around-the-clock.

You're a stupid man, Connor. You were handed a gift of a lifetime and you threw it all away. You thought you were being some kind of heroic martyr for letting Jazelle go. But you're actually a fool. A jerk. And a coward.

The condemning voice going off in Connor's ear was suddenly interrupted as Joseph climbed back into the truck and tossed a brown paper bag toward him.

"See if those will put you in a better mood," Joseph told him.

Connor opened the sack and, after handing one of tacos to Joseph, pulled one out for himself. Normally, the delicious aroma of eggs and chorizo sausage would have his mouth watering. Instead, his stomach revolted and clenched into a hard knot.

"Sorry, Joe," he apologized. "Go ahead and tell

me that I'm being a jerk. I know I am. But I...don't know what to do."

In the middle of unwrapping the waxed paper from the taco, Joseph paused long enough to level a tired look at him. "You don't? Well, I sure as hell know! The way I see it, Connor, you have two choices. You pull out your phone and you call one of those girlfriends of yours and make a date. You go out with the woman and forget about Jazelle.

"If that idea doesn't appeal to you, then you call Jazelle, beg her to forgive you, and confess that you can't live without her. And if you're lucky, she'll give you another chance."

"You think it's that simple, huh? Well, it isn't," Connor told him then forced himself to bite into the taco.

"Nothing is simple about making a commitment, Connor. Before you ever asked Jazelle for a date, I tried to warn you that she was different. That you ought to stay away from her."

"Yeah. I remember. I should've listened."

Rolling his eyes, Joseph continued. "When you didn't heed my warning, I tried to be hopeful. I honestly wanted to think that Jazelle was the woman who could turn your life around. I was wrong. You don't want to be turned around. And it looks like you don't want her, either."

Don't want her? If I live to be a hundred, I'll still want her, Connor thought miserably.

"I'm no good, Joe. I don't have to tell you that."

Joseph dug another taco out of the paper bag. "You *are* good, Connor. Once you realize that, you won't have any problem telling Jazelle you love her."

Love her? All of Connor's life, he'd shunned the word, the very thought of caring that much for someone, or having someone care that much for him. Even as a child, he'd never heard the word spoken to him. His father had expressed his love for Connor by comforting him, guiding and sheltering him, but he'd never actually heard the man say *I love you, son.* Up until he'd met Jazelle, Connor hadn't really believed he could feel that much emotion. But he did. And trying to deny it wasn't making it go away.

"I do want her, Joe. I want her and Raine more than you can imagine. But when I get to thinking about the three of us as a family, I get sick with fear. I think about all the mistakes I might make."

Joe snorted. "You think Tessa and I are perfect? There is no perfect, Connor. Don't be worrying about the mistakes you *might* make. You need to concentrate on the one you're making right now."

Later that day, Connor and Joseph were back in their office at Prescott, writing up reports before they finished their shift, when Connor's cell phone rang.

He started to ignore the call then, deciding it could be important, pulled the phone from his shirt pocket.

Seeing Jazelle's number on the ID stunned him. Why would she be calling? Was something wrong with her? Or Raine? No, he'd be the last person she'd contact, he decided.

He cleared his throat and punched the accept button. "Hello?"

"Hi, Connor! Do you know who this is?"

All sorts of questions suddenly darted through Connor's head. "Yes, I do. It's Raine."

A mischievous giggle came back at him.

"I got Mommy's phone when she wasn't looking. She lets me call Little Joe sometimes, so I know how. I found your number and punched it."

The sound of Raine's precious voice brought a lump to Connor's throat. He'd missed the boy. Very nearly as much as he'd missed Jazelle. "So I see. Uh, does your mommy know you have the phone now?"

"No. She's doing something with a mop—in the big den. Grandma Reeva said we could go home, but Mommy didn't want to go home. She says she has to get things ready for visitors."

"Oh. So you and your mommy are at Three Rivers," he said then glanced over to Joseph's desk to see his partner was staring curiously at him. No doubt he was just as surprised as Connor was that Raine had called him.

"Yeah. We'll probably be here a long time, but that's okay. Nick is going to let me look at his arrowhead collection. He has bunches of good ones. Him and Hannah find them on the res. Maybe me and you could go there sometime. Hannah's grandma has chickens. They're funny, too. They flap their wings and cluck."

Connor asked, "You've been to the res before?"

"Uh-huh. Sometimes when Mommy is in a happy mood, she lets me go there with Nick. But she hasn't been too happy here lately."

Connor felt like a hand had shoved its way into his chest and was squeezing every drop of blood from his heart. With everything inside him, he wished he could reach through the phone and hug the child to his breast.

Before Connor could assemble some sort of suitable reply, Raine suddenly announced, "My birthday is gonna be in two days. I'll be six years old then. Do you know what that means?"

Clueless, Connor answered, "That you're going to be six."

More giggles sounded in his ear. "I'm gonna be in first grade! That's what it means."

"Oh. First grade. Wow! You'll be going to big school then."

"Yeah. Kindergarten was fun, but first grade will be funner. I'll learn how to read more words and then I can read a book to Mommy. She'll like that."

Connor was forced to clear his throat again. "Yes, she'll like that very much."

"I'm gonna have a birthday party at the ranch, too," he said proudly. "Grandma Reeva is making me a giant cake so everyone can have lots to eat. And some orange punch, 'cause orange is my favorite. And guess what? Holt is gonna let me ride a real ranch horse—not just a pony, either. A big horse! Mommy's worried, but Holt laughed at her. He says the kid is six. He should've been riding a big horse three years ago."

Connor couldn't help but smile at that. "I'm sure Holt is right. Sounds like you're going to have lots of fun at your party."

"Yeah. But it won't be any fun if you don't come, too, Connor. Will you?"

Go to Three Rivers and face Jazelle? As soon as he laid eyes on her, he'd want to pull her into his arms. He'd want to pour out his heart and pray that she would understand.

"Uh, you're inviting me to your party?"

"Yeah! I want you to come! Really bad."

And Connor wanted to go "really bad," he suddenly realized. He didn't want to disappoint this child. Not for any reason. "Then I'll be there. I promise."

"Yippee! This is gonna be the best birthday ever!" he practically shouted but suddenly lowered his voice to a hushed tone. "Uh-oh! I think I hear Mommy coming. I gotta put her phone back on the cabinet or I'm gonna be in big trouble. 'Bye, Connor!"

The connection went dead and Connor thoughtfully slipped the phone back into his shirt pocket. Across the room, Joseph poured himself a cup of coffee.

"What was that about?" he asked.

"Raine apparently got his mother's phone without her knowing and called me. To invite me to his birthday party out at Three Rivers."

Joseph nodded. "I knew about the party. Little Joe is already talking about going. He loves to play with Raine and the idea of gifts and cake makes the whole event even more exciting."

Before Jazelle and Raine had come into his life, the subject of kids and birthday parties would've bored Connor to tears. Now he felt excluded because Joseph hadn't shared the information with him. How had this change in him happened?

"You haven't mentioned to me that Raine was having a birthday."

Joseph said, "Kid stuff isn't your thing. Besides, you've put him and Jazelle out of your life. Haven't you?"

Connor looked at him and suddenly it was like he'd been hit by lightning and he was seeing everything with crystal-clear vision. "No. I haven't. Hearing Raine's voice—oh, God, you're right, Joe," he said, his voice cracking with emotion. "It's all very simple. I want Jazelle and Raine in my life. I don't want to lose them."

"It's about damned time I heard you say that." He poured a second cup of coffee and carried it over to Connor. "Here, drink up and finish your report. Then you're going to come up with a plan to convince Jazelle that you're a changed man."

Could he convince her of that? He had to, Connor

thought. Otherwise, his future would be nothing but a gray, lonely road to nowhere.

Later that night, Connor was sitting at the kitchen table, staring at his phone and trying to decide whether he should call Jazelle or simply drive to her house and surprise her.

The latter would probably better, he thought. At least that way he could catch her off guard and, hopefully, plead his case before she had time to think too hard on the matter.

What the hell, Connor, you want the woman to be certain of her feelings. And you want her to realize on her own that the two of you belong together. Not because you pressured or tricked her. Go to her, lay your heart out, and just see what happens.

For once Connor agreed with the voice in his head and, with that decision made, he headed to the bedroom for a clean shirt. Halfway there, he paused at the sound of a vehicle pulling to a stop in front of the house.

Living on the outskirts of Wilhoit, Connor rarely had visitors and those were mostly locals who knew he was a deputy and wanted him to go arrest someone they'd been feuding with. He wasn't ready to deal with such nonsense tonight.

Turning on his heel, he went to the door and stepped onto the porch. The yard light illuminated most of the small lawn and part of his truck, which was parked at the north side of the house. Behind the truck was an older red truck that looked… Oh, Lord, it was Jazelle!

His heart chugging heavily in his chest, he walked down the steps and out to meet her. By the time he reached her vehicle, she was already standing on the ground, waiting for him.

"Hello, Connor."

He stepped closer as questions swirled inside his head. "Jazelle, what—how did you find my house? You've never been here before."

She smiled faintly and, as Connor's gaze roamed over her, he realized he'd never seen anything so beautiful in his life. The sight of her was like the welcome vision of a rainbow after a terrible storm.

"Joe and Tessa gave me directions and I took a chance that you'd be here."

"Oh." He peered at her truck, but the interior light had already gone off, making it impossible for him to see inside. "Where's Raine? Didn't he come with you?"

"He's at the Bar X, playing with Little Joe. Tessa and Joe offered to watch him while I came up here to see you."

She didn't sound angry or bitter. But he didn't detect any cheerfulness, either. Did she come all this way just to give him another robot act? he wondered. What was she doing here?

"I see," he said, even though he didn't. "Well, uh, would you like to go in?"

"I would. Unless I'm interrupting something important."

The only important thing to Connor was making her understand just how much he loved her. And though, he wanted to yank her into his arms and kiss the breath out of her, he figured that wasn't the right way to go about it.

"You're not interrupting." Clasping a hand around her upper arm, he urged her toward the house. "The ground is uneven, so watch your step. Something has been burrowing holes in the yard."

She didn't say anything and as they made their way onto the porch and into the house, Connor feared this visit might prove to be even more painful than the last one. If so, he didn't think he could survive it.

Inside the living room, Jazelle stood in the middle of the room while Connor turned on a pair of lamps. As she gazed at the serviceable furniture and the clutter of beer bottles, coffee cups and piles of paper files scattered around, he could only imagine what she was thinking.

"Sit anywhere you like," he said as he picked up a pair of cowboy boots lying in front of the couch and set them out of the way. "Sorry about the mess. We've been working overtime and I'm not too good of a housekeeper."

"No need to apologize," she said as she sank onto the middle of the couch.

"Would you like coffee or a soda?" he offered.

"No, thanks. I just need to say what I came to say."

Something that couldn't have been said over the phone? Like what?

Biting back the questions, he dared to take a seat next to her. "I'm a little confused, Jazelle. Is something wrong with Raine?"

A pained look came over her face. "No. Raine is perfectly fine."

He let out a breath of relief. "Then you forgot to tell me something the last time we talked?"

"I don't want to think about the last time we talked," she said bluntly. "That wasn't a pleasant time for me. And, frankly, I've been in a horrible state ever since."

What was she trying to say? That splitting from him had made her miserable? Or was he reading far too much in her words?

If possible, his heart thumped even faster. "I haven't exactly been…happy," he told her, thinking that was the understatement of the century. These past few days he hadn't even been human.

Her nostrils flared as she drew in a deep breath and Connor noticed she looked unusually pale and drawn. The idea that she'd been suffering over anything made him want to pull her into his arms and simply hold her tight.

She said, "Uh, this evening I was checking my phone for any missed calls and I figured out that Raine had been talking with you. I want to apologize for that."

"Why? You don't want him to talk with me?"

She groaned. "I don't mind if he talks to you. But… I don't want him bothering you. Especially if you're at work."

"He wasn't bothering me. I enjoyed our talk." How could he explain that just the sound of the child's voice had jerked Connor out of the miserable fog he'd been living in?

Her gaze lifted to his and Connor suddenly felt like his insides were melting to a worthless puddle of nothing.

"You did?"

"Yes, I did. He invited me to his birthday party."

She blew out a long breath. "I know. That's the main reason I'm here. I realize my son put you on the spot and I'm sorry about that. I know you told him you'd come to the party, but you really don't have to. I'll make some excuse for you not being there."

At that moment every doubt, every fear, Connor had ever felt about being a husband and father drained out of him and as he looked into Jazelle's blue eyes he was amazed at how clearly he could see the three of them together as a family.

"No," he said firmly. "Raine doesn't need excuses. He needs me."

Her mouth fell open. "You? What does that mean?"

His hands gently clasped her shoulders. "Raine needs me as his father. And I hope—I pray—that you need me as your husband."

Shock glazed her eyes and then her head turned

back and forth with disbelief. "Husband? Connor—
what are you saying?"

"That I love you. That I want you to be my wife.
That I want Raine to be our son and I want us to
give him siblings."

She jumped to her feet and covered her face with
both hands. "Why are you saying this to me now?
Is this some sort of cruel joke?"

Rising, Connor gently pulled her into the circle of
his arms. "I've never been more serious in my life,
Jazelle. You'll probably find this hard to believe, but
before you drove up, I was getting ready to drive
down to your place and plead for you to forgive me."

Tilting her head back, she looked up at him. "Forgive you? For what?"

"For being a dope, a jerk, a coward and several
more things, including idiot. The other night when
we agreed to call it quits, I knew deep down that I
was lying to you—to myself. I knew then that you
and Raine had become my life and I didn't want to
lose you—but I went on with that silly agreement
because I thought it was the right and smart thing
to do. And you seemed determined that…well…you
didn't want me around anymore. I don't blame you
if you still feel that way. But I'm hoping you were
doing a bit of lying yourself that night."

Tears filled her eyes and rolled unheeded down
her face. "Oh, Connor, I didn't mean a word I was
saying. All along, I had to fight to keep from throwing my arms around you and telling you how much

I loved you. How much I wanted you to believe in yourself and in me.

"This afternoon, Maureen made me promise that I'd have a talk with you and tell you that I'd give you the time you needed to get used to the idea of being a family man." A radiant smile suddenly spread across her face. "I always knew she was a wise woman, I just never realized how wise until now."

With his hands against her back, he drew her tighter to him. "Joe said something to me this morning that struck hard. He said that he and Tessa weren't perfect. That there was no perfect."

"Smart man," Jazelle said. "They're not perfect, but they're happy and that's what I want us to be, Connor. We'll both make mistakes. That's to be expected because we're human. But we'll figure them out—together."

"Together. That's a very beautiful word. Almost as beautiful as you, my darling." He lowered his head to hers and let his lips convey all the aching loneliness he'd felt these past days without her, and all the love he promised to give her in the future. "You know, I think Raine's birthday party would be the perfect time to announce our engagement. If you can get away from work tomorrow, we'll drive up to Prescott and find a ring."

Her eyes glowed up at him. "I don't need a fancy ring, Connor. Anything will do just as long as you put it on my finger."

"Say, you've just given me an idea. The Broken

Spur has some trinket machines," he teased. "I think I can spare a few quarters until we get one with a ring. They're adjustable, too. So we won't have to worry about sizing."

Laughing, she hugged him tightly. "Reeva and the Hollisters are going to be thrilled for us. But not nearly as much as Raine will be when he hears you're going to be his daddy. What a birthday gift that's going to be." A sly smile on her face, she began to unbutton his shirt. "Right now, I think you and I should make the most of this quiet time, don't you?"

Chuckling under his breath, he lowered his lips to hers. "And take advantage of our babysitters?"

She smiled against his kiss. "I don't think Joe and Tessa will mind at all."

Epilogue

Six weeks later, on a cold October night, the den in the Three Rivers Ranch house was filled with family and friends enjoying appetizers, drinks and plenty of conversation. Normally, Jazelle would be scurrying here and there, making sure everyone had their favorite cocktail in hand, but tonight was different. Tonight she and Connor were the guests of honor.

"I honestly don't know why Maureen insisted on giving us a rehearsal dinner for our wedding tomorrow," Jazelle told Connor as they stood to one side of the crackling fire in the massive fireplace. "We didn't even have a rehearsal. And she's gone to the expense of hiring outside help to deal with tonight and the reception tomorrow."

"We didn't need a rehearsal," Connor said with a grin, his gaze traveling over the beautiful image she made in an emerald-green dress, her blond hair coiled into an elegant chignon. "All we're going to do is stand in front of the minister and repeat our vows. Tessa will be your maid of honor, Joe is my best man, and Raine, the ring bearer. Everyone already knows their part."

Connor made it sound simple, but in truth, Maureen and her daughters-in-law had put hours of work into planning the wedding, not to mention the expense. The event would take place tomorrow at two o'clock in Wickenburg at the small church Jazelle had attended since childhood. Afterward, the married couple and the wedding guests would return here to Three Rivers for a reception complete with plenty of champagne, a massive five-tiered cake Reeva had already baked, and a live band for dancing.

"To be honest, Connor, I'm overwhelmed by the generosity of the Hollisters. It wasn't their place to do all of this for us."

Snaking an arm around the back of her waist, Connor hugged her close to his side. "No. But they see us as family. And they want this time for us to be special."

It couldn't be more special, Jazelle thought as she glanced around the room at everyone who'd come to celebrate with them. Even her father and his family had driven up from Oracle to be there for the special day. Unfortunately, her mother had refused to

attend any of the wedding events. She was still la-
beling Jazelle a fool for marrying a man who wore
a badge and set himself up as a target.

As though Connor could read her thoughts, he
said, "I'm glad your father was able to be here with
you. I was thinking I wouldn't like him. But I do.
He seems like a stand-up guy."

"He's like the rest of us, Connor, he's not perfect,
but he tries. I think that's why Mom is so bitter. She
hates herself for letting him slip away."

"You could be right," he said. "I'm just sorry she
made the choice to not be with you at such a special
time in your life. I hope that doesn't make you sad."

She shook her head. "Her stubbornness isn't going
to make me sad. Tomorrow we'll be married. So
if I'm acting giddy, don't blame it on my cocktail.
You're the reason I can't stop smiling."

He bent his head just enough to press a kiss on
her cheek. "Joe's been accusing me of going around
with a goofy grin on my face. Not exactly the ap-
propriate expression when you're dealing with law-
breakers, but I can't help it. Ever since you agreed to
marry me, I've been walking on a cloud."

She said, "Speaking of Joe and Tessa, I'm still
blown away with their plans for us. Who builds
someone a house for a wedding gift?"

As soon as the couple had learned Jazelle and
Connor were engaged, they had immediately begun
making plans to build them a house on the Bar X,
not far from their own ranch house. They reasoned

that Jazelle needed to be close to her work on Three Rivers, and with Connor and Joseph being partners, it would also be a perfect setup for their jobs. Not to mention the added benefit of having Raine and Little Joe grow up close together.

Connor shook his head. "I've learned long ago not to argue with Joe. I can't win. But what he doesn't know is that you and I will eventually pay them back for the cost of the house. I realize he and Tessa are wealthy and they also have plenty of land to spare, but that makes no difference. I want for us to pay our own way."

She said, "It's not money they want from us, Connor. All they want is for us to share our happiness and our lives with them."

"That will be easy enough to do."

He was nuzzling another kiss on her cheek when Emily-Ann and Taggart walked up to join them.

Jazelle quickly hugged her very pregnant friend. "I'm so glad you felt like coming tonight, Emily-Ann," she told her. "I hope you can make it to the wedding tomorrow."

Taggart settled a loving smile on his wife's face. "She's worried her water will break in front of everyone. I told her no one cares about that. We all just want the little guy to get here safely."

"Or little girl," Emily-Ann corrected him then, laughing, placed a hand on top of her rounded belly. "Right now I feel like there're two babies kicking around in there."

"Emily-Ann, I hope to heck that's not a screwdriver you're sipping on," Blake said as he and Joseph joined the group.

Rolling her eyes at the ranch manager, Emily-Ann held up the fluted glass. "Pure orange juice without so much as a sprinkle of sugar," she assured him.

"Good. I want my godchild to be healthy and strong." Blake winked at Taggart then turned his attention to Connor. "How's the husband-to-be holding up?"

Joseph let out a good-natured groan. "Do you need to ask, brother? Connor is going to wear that goofy grin for the rest of his life."

The laughter around the happy group was suddenly interrupted with the ring of Joseph's cell phone.

"Don't answer it, Joe," Blake teased. "You and Connor might have to go to work."

Ignoring him, Joseph pulled the phone out and, after one glance at the ID, promptly answered the call.

"Yes, this is Joseph Hollister," he said to the person on the other end. "Yes, I remember. We've been hoping to hear from you."

Sensing the call might be important, everyone in the group began to exchange curious glances.

After a short pause, Joseph said, "Yes. We can do that. Take whatever time you need. Just call me when you're ready. Yes. And thank you."

Joseph hung up the phone and turned a stunned

look on the group clustered around him. "This is amazing," he said. "I'm celebrating my best friend's upcoming nuptials and now this call. It has to be a sign of good things to come."

Still grinning, Connor asked, "What? The two of us are being promoted?"

"Even better," Joe answered. "That was Ginny Patterson on the phone. Seems as though she's had a change of heart and she's ready to talk with us."

"No joke?" Blake asked with disbelief.

"I'm serious," Joseph said.

Connor looked hopefully at his partner. "When? What did she say?"

"She needs to figure out somewhere safe to meet with us. As soon as she does, she'll give us a call."

Connor and Jazelle exchanged pointed glances.

Blake looked astonished. "She doesn't feel safe with two deputies?"

"Apparently not," Joseph replied.

Jazelle's gaze traveled across the large room to where Gil and Maureen were sitting with their heads close together. "This might change everything for those two," she said. Wrapping her arm through Connor's, she smiled into his blue eyes. "Let's hope they're going to be happy. As happy as we are right now."

Lifting his glass high, Blake toasted her wish. "Hear, hear."

Everyone sipped from their glasses and then she felt Connor's fingers tighten on the side of her waist, reminding her that tomorrow they would become husband and wife. Tomorrow, and all the days afterward, they both would have the family they'd never had before. And that was a mighty heady feeling.

* * * * *

*Look for the next book in the Men of the West
miniseries, coming from Harlequin Special
Edition
in March 2021!*

*And in the meantime, try more of great
single parent romances:*

A Matchmaker's Challenge
By Teresa Southwick

The Single Mom's Second Chance
By Kathy Douglass

A Family for a Week
By Melissa Senate

*Available now wherever Harlequin Special Edition
books and ebooks are sold!*

COMING NEXT MONTH FROM

♦ HARLEQUIN
SPECIAL EDITION

Available August 18, 2020

#2785 THE MAVERICK'S BABY ARRANGEMENT
Montana Mavericks: What Happened to Beatrix?
by Kathy Douglass

In order to retain custody of his eight-month-old niece, Daniel Dubois convinces event planner and confirmed businesswoman Brittany Brandt to marry him. It's only supposed to be a mutually beneficial business agreement...*if* they can both keep their hearts out of the equation.

#2786 THE LAST MAN SHE EXPECTED
Welcome to Starlight • by Michelle Major

When Mara Reed agrees to partner with her sworn enemy, Parker Johnson, to help a close friend, she doesn't expect the feelings of love and tenderness that complicate every interaction with the handsome attorney. Will Mara and Parker risk everything for love?

#2787 CHANGING HIS PLANS
Gallant Lake Stories • by Jo McNally

Real estate developer Brittany Doyle is eager to bring the mountain town of Gallant Lake into the twenty-first century...by changing everything. Hardware store owner Nate Thomas hates change. These opposites refuse to compromise, except when it comes to falling in love.

#2788 A WINNING SEASON
Wickham Falls Weddings • by Rochelle Alers

When Sutton Reed returns to Wickham Falls after finishing a successful baseball career, he assumes he'll just join the family business and live an uneventful life. Until his neighbor's younger brother tries to steal his car, that is. Now he's finding himself mentoring the boy—and being drawn to Zoey Allen like no one else.

#2789 IN SERVICE OF LOVE
Sutter Creek, Montana • by Laurel Greer

Commitmentphobic veterinarian Maggie is focused on training a Great Dane as a service dog and expanding the family dog-training business. Can widowed single dad Asher's belief in love after loss inspire Maggie to risk her heart and find forever with the irresistible librarian?

#2790 THE SLOW BURN
Masterson, Texas • by Caro Carson

When firefighter Caden Sterling unexpectedly delivers Tana McKenna's baby by the side of the road, the unlikely threesome forms a special bond. Their flirty friendship slowly becomes more, until Tana's ex and the truth about her baby catches up with her. Can she win back the only man who can make this family complete?

YOU CAN FIND MORE INFORMATION ON UPCOMING HARLEQUIN TITLES, FREE EXCERPTS AND MORE AT HARLEQUIN.COM.

HSECNM0820

He stuck his head around the corner of the fasteners
aisle just in time to see a tall brunette stagger into the
revolving seed display. Some of the packets went flying,
but she managed to steady the display before the whole
thing toppled. He took in what probably had been a very
nice silk blouse and tailored trouser suit before she was
drenched in the storm raging outside. The heel on one of
the ridiculously high heels she was wearing had snapped
off, explaining why she was stumbling around.

"Having a bad morning?"

The woman looked up in annoyance, strands of dark,
wet hair falling across her face.

"You could say that. I don't suppose you have a shoe
repair place in this town?" She looked at the bright red
heel in her hand.

Nate shook his head as he approached her. "Nope. But hand it over. I'll see what I can do."

A perfectly shaped brow arched high. "Why? Are you going to cobble them back together with—" she gestured around widely "—maybe some staples or screws?"

"Technically, what you just described is the definition of cobbling, so yeah. I've got some glue that'll do the trick." He met her gaze calmly. "It'd be a lot easier to do if you'd take the shoe off. Unless you also think I'm a blacksmith?"

He was teasing her. Something about this soaking-wet woman still having so much...regal bearing...amused Nate. He wasn't usually a fan of the pearl-clutching country club set who strutted through Gallant Lake on the weekends and referred to his family's hardware store as "adorable." But he couldn't help admiring this woman's ability to hold on to her superiority while looking like she accidentally went to a water park instead of the business meeting she was dressed for. To be honest, he also admired the figure that expensive red suit was clinging to as it dripped water on his floor.

He held out his hand. "I'm Nate Thomas. This is my store."

She let out an irritated sigh. "Brittany Doyle." She slid her long, slender hand into his and gripped with surprising strength. He held it for just a half second longer than necessary before shaking off the odd current of interest she invoked in him.

Don't miss
Changing His Plans *by Jo McNally,*
available September 2020 wherever
Harlequin Special Edition books and ebooks are sold.

Harlequin.com

HSEEXP0820

Love Harlequin romance?

DISCOVER.

Be the first to find out about promotions,
news and exclusive content!

 Facebook.com/HarlequinBooks

Twitter.com/HarlequinBooks

Instagram.com/HarlequinBooks

Pinterest.com/HarlequinBooks

ReaderService.com

EXPLORE.

Sign up for the Harlequin e-newsletter and
download a free book from any series at
TryHarlequin.com

CONNECT.

Join our Harlequin community to
share your thoughts and connect
with other romance readers!
Facebook.com/groups/HarlequinConnection

HSOCIAL2020